Advent and Christmas Stories

A treasury

of stories, verses

and songs

Hawthorn Press

Published by Hawthorn Press, Hawthorn House,
1 Lansdown Lane, Stroud, Gloucestershire, GL5 1BJ, UK
Tel: (01453) 757040
Email: info@hawthornpress.com, Website: www.hawthornpress.com

Cover illustration © Toyonobu
Illustrations by Marije Rowling
Design and layout by Lucy Guenot
Reprinted by CMP Books, Poole, UK 2025

Printed on environmentally friendly chlorine-free paper sourced from renewable forest stock.

This product complies with the requirements of the following EU regulation: General Product Safety Regulation (GPSR) 2023/988

British Library Cataloguing in Publication Data applied for
ISBN 978-1-907359-25-5

Advent and Christmas Stories

A treasury
of stories, verses
and songs

Estelle Bryer and Janni Nicol

Illustrations by Marije Rowling

Hawthorn Press

Contents

DEDICATION

To Jason, Emma, Nicholas and Alexandra,
and all the children whose cries of 'more'
and 'again' have inspired us.

Foreword

Storytelling offers refuge and nurture within family life. Many families throughout the world today are sharing in a revival of this household art, and finding that it counters the forces that would divide us from each other and fragment our lives.

Estelle Bryer and Janni Nicol offer us Christmas stories that create a peaceful, enfolding space for ourselves and our children, where wonder can do its healing work. Each of these tales inspires us to take a deep, fulfilling breath of imagination and let Christmas radiance grow in our eyes, words and hearts. They lead us beyond the ordinary laws of nature into the truth of miracles and wonders: we discover the holiness of rabbits and birds, turtles and trees as they guide and protect the holy family.

The authors invite us to learn to tell these stories by heart, so that they grow truly alive in us, in the same spirit that we might make a gift with our own hands. Such a gift is always more precious and more individual than one bought in a shop. In telling these gentle and compelling little tales, the gift of storytelling can sustain us and weave its golden threads from heart to heart.

Nancy Mellon
School of Therapeutic Storytelling
New Hampshire, USA

Introduction

Every family knows that young children enhance our celebration of Christmas: their natural sense of wonder pervades the home, creating a special Christmas mood.

The stories contained in this book help engender a sense of wonder and reverence at Christmas, particularly for children between the ages of three and seven. They have been told for many years in kindergartens, and at home to the authors' children and grandchildren. Like most stories passed down in the oral tradition, they have many and varied sources (see below).

The stories take us through Advent to Christmas, and on into the time of the holy family's flight into Egypt. These last stories, in fact, can be told throughout the year. The children particularly love this last section, as they delight in the way that the whole of nature collaborates in hoodwinking the pursuers.

The Nativity story is told in verse form. This can be used also to accompany standing table top figures, which you move according to the story, or narrated to support a little simple play acted by children or adults. Bits can be added, or left out according to need (and time).

There are other stories here not necessarily about the holy family, yet still connected with Christmas – such as those about the fir tree. Children love to hear these while quietly sitting by the Christmas tree in the evening, admiring its twinkling lights.

These stories are written specifically for reading aloud or, even better, for telling. Many people think telling stories from memory is difficult, and don't even try – but it becomes so much easier with experience. Telling a story without looking at the book brings the story alive – and you can add little details of your own, perhaps, that are just right for the special children in front of you! Before telling a story it is always better, if possible, to read it through carefully and memorise the essentials.

If possible, try not to dramatise too much when telling or reading stories to this age group. Keeping your voice neutral, and not using different accents or tones for the different characters or circumstances, leaves young children freer to use their own imagination. At this age too much emphasis can overwhelm them and hinder them from creating their own images. After the age of seven or so, drama and characterisation become much more important.

Some of the stories seem to overlap or even contradict each other but young children do not notice this, for they love repetition and do not analyse things as adults do. The important thing in a story is the mood or atmosphere it conveys.

Wherever possible we have tried to ascertain the sources of the stories; but in many cases their origin seems to have been forgotten over the course of time. As they have been told and retold over the years in many different kindergartens and homes, the stories have gradually developed and changed.

We hope that you enjoy these stories and that in your family they become as much a source of pleasure and sustaining tradition as they have in ours.

For further information on storytelling, see: *Storytelling with Children* by Nancy Mellon, Hawthorn Press 2000.

We know that some of the stories originated from Hermien Ijzerman in Europe and were translated from German by Janine Hurner in Cape Town.

Janine and Estelle worked together in order to develop the Nativity play (*The Christmas Story in Verse and Song*, page 21) for their kindergarten children in Cape Town in 1965, as a performance for the parents. It has been performed since then not only as a play, but as story puppet play, family play, and in many countries throughout the world.

A few stories have been greatly adapted and changed in the retelling over many years, but we have traced the origins of: *The Fir Tree* which is adapted from a story by Hans Christian Andersen; *The Wise Men's Well* and *The Torch* from Selma Lagerlof; *The Camel* from Jill Taplin and *The White Bird* from N.Wood.

As to the others... we don't know any more! If we have failed to mention any of the original authors we apologise, but are ever grateful to you...

Christmas Verse

Gentle Jesus, meek and mild,
Look upon this little child.
Make me gentle as Thou art,
Come and live within my heart.
Take my childish hand in Thine,
Guide these little feet of mine,
So shall all my happy days
Sing their merry song of praise,
And the world will always see
Christ, the holy child, in me.

The Annunciation

There was once a little garden where there were beautiful flowers, big shining rocks, a little bush and a deep well. But sister Rain did not come to this little garden for such a long time that all the flowers dried up and died, and the grass shrivelled up so that there was nothing green left in the whole garden. Even the water in the well dried up, leaving not one drop for the little water nixies to swim in.

Then all the light went out of the rocks and they became very sad and cold and hard. The little bush became so dry and thirsty that it grew nasty and put out sharp thorns, saying: 'I am going to prick anyone who comes near me!' No one wanted to come into that garden anymore.

Now in a little house nearby there lived a young maiden who was so beautiful that wherever she walked the flowers bowed down and kissed her feet, and the trees threw down their most beautiful leaves to make a soft path for her to walk on. Everyone who saw her loved her, her heart was as pure as snow, and her name was Mary.

One day Mary came into the garden, and when she saw how dry and dead everything was her heart grew sad. She looked into the well and saw that it was dry and empty. Then she looked at the little bush, and she saw that it was thirsty, and two tears rolled down her cheeks and dropped into the bottom of the well, and she looked at the rocks and she saw how dark and sad they were. She went up to the little thorn bush, and the thorn bush said: 'Ha, I am going to prick her,' but when it looked into her kind and beautiful eyes it pulled its thorns in and said: 'This maiden I could never harm.'

Then Mary went down on her knees and put her hands together to pray for the little garden. She prayed for the rocks and she prayed for the thorn bush and she prayed for the little water nixies and she prayed for the flowers. While she was praying a great shining light came into the garden. Mary opened her eyes and looked up. There, standing in front of her, was a shining angel dressed all in white, holding a white lily in his hand. In a beautiful voice he said to her: 'Blessed art thou among women, for thou shalt have a child and he will be the heavenly shining child and thou shalt call his name Jesus.' Then the angel went away.

Mary stood up and looked into the well, and there, where her two tears had fallen, water started to bubble up. The water nixies shouted with joy and jumped into the water. Soon the well was full and Mary took some water to feed the little thorn bush. She stroked the thorns and as she touched them they turned into roses with the softest petals and the sweetest scent. She went to the cold grey rocks and as she stroked them the light started to shine from them again.

Then everywhere flowers started growing, and the whole garden was singing. The little water nixies were singing 'Gloria', the roses were singing 'Gloria', even the rocks were singing 'Gloria' in deep rock voices, and all the air was filled with singing, singing and still more singing.

Mary's Wedding

And now the time came for Mary to be married. From far and wide men came who wished to marry her, for she was known to be good, pure and beautiful. Mary had a little branch from a tree, and when each man came to the house she said: 'Hold this branch, and if leaves should grow from it while you are holding it, then you are the one who is chosen to marry me.'

One after the other the young men held the branch in their hands, but nothing grew, so they had to go away.

One day an older man, a kindly and good man, came to shelter at Mary's house. When he saw Mary he loved her and wished to marry her. Mary gave him the branch to hold, and as he held it leaves started to grow from it, and Mary knew: 'This is the man who is chosen to be my husband.' His name was Joseph; and Mary and Joseph were married.

Now the whole village began to prepare for the wedding. The weavers and tailors made a special cloak for Joseph to wear and the hatters made him a special hat. There was baking of breads and cakes, and the making of flower garlands. Mary's crown of roses and lilies was woven. Long tables were covered with white cloths and the musicians tuned their instruments. A golden ring was forged, which Mary, as a married woman, would wear on the forefinger of her right hand.

Mary chose to be married in the Forgotten Garden. The people led her out of the village holding the flower garlands on high. The cuckoo and the pigeon, which lived close to Mary, flew in excitement from her to the waiting Joseph and back again. They sang as they flew, filling the air with music.

In the garden the canopy was held atop its four poles, covering Mary and Joseph like the roof of the home they would share.

Joseph promised that he would love and care for Mary as long as he lived, and then he put the ring on Mary's finger. Mary promised that she would love and care for Joseph as long as she lived, and she gave him such a sweet smile that he thought his heart would melt.

A glass was put on the ground in front of Joseph, and he crushed it under his heel and said: 'The love people have for one another can break as easily as this glass if they do not cherish each other. We will care for each other with gentleness as we would the finest crystal glass.'

Then they held hands and turned to the people who clapped and cheered, and Mary and Joseph were led back through the flower garlands. Music began to play and there was dancing and singing and feasting throughout the village in celebration of the marriage of Mary and Joseph.

Joseph was a carpenter. He was the finest carpenter. He had strength in his hands and arms from sawing and planing and sanding the furniture that he made. Strong hands which could also do the finest carving and painting on his furniture – painting so fine that sometimes he used a brush with only three cat's hairs!

His furniture was smooth to touch, his furniture was beautiful to look at, his furniture was so strong it would last a lifetime.

Everyone wanted Joseph's furniture!

Secretly, before the wedding, while the people of the village were busy, Joseph had made a cupboard for Mary. It had two doors and broad shelves inside. On the one door he had carved 'Mary' and on the other 'Joseph'; and the names were surrounded with hearts, flowers and birds. Lightly he painted them and waxed and polished the wood, so that when he took Mary to their house after the wedding and lit the lamps, it glowed in the corner like a jewel. Mary stood before it and she stroked it. 'Oh, thank you,' she said.

So Mary and Joseph settled down together, and every day Mary dusted and polished the cupboard.

One day Joseph said: 'Mary, I will make the finest cradle for the baby to sleep in when he arrives. It will have rockers and carvings. It will be made with my love, so that he will sleep peacefully.'

And that is what Joseph did.

Mary and Joseph

After Mary and Joseph were married, they lived in a little town called Nazareth. One day, soldiers came riding into the town and they had big drums on which they were beating. The captain called out in a loud voice: 'All the people in this town must come to Bethlehem to be counted.'

So Mary and Joseph had to go to Bethlehem. By now Mary was quite big with her child who was soon to be born, and so Joseph found a little donkey to carry her. Mary sat on the donkey and Joseph walked by her side leading it. There were many, many people on the road, all going to Bethlehem to be counted. Mary said: 'Poor donkey, you must be tired, I will walk for a while so that you can rest.' The donkey was pleased to rest although he loved to carry Mary on his back.

As they were walking along they saw a big rock, with hard sharp edges, standing right in the middle of the road. That rock once shone with a light of its own, but now it was dark and no one came to sit on it for if they did it would cut them. Next to the rock was a big thorn bush that once had flowers, but now no more flowers grew on it, so it became nasty and sad and pricked everyone who came past. The rock and the thorn bush were so big that they almost blocked the road; so everyone had to walk a long way to go around them.

When Mary and Joseph came up to the big rock, Mary was tired and wanted to sit down. When the rock felt Mary sit on it, a warm glow started to go right through it and so it shifted a little to make a little seat for Mary so that she could be comfortable. So there Mary sat, and when she had rested she stood up and turned to look at the thorn bush. The thorn bush shivered and thought: 'This lady is so beautiful, for her I would do anything,' and she opened up for Mary and Joseph and the donkey to pass through. Mary thanked the thorn bush, and the thorn bush felt so warm and full of love that soft pink roses started to grow all over it.

That night Mary and Joseph came to the town of Bethlehem. There were many people there from all over the country, all looking for a place to stay. They went from house to house to ask if there was any room to sleep, but all the rooms were full, and the reply was always the same: 'There is no room in here!'

At last they came to a little farmhouse. Joseph knocked at the door and the farmer opened it and said: 'I am sorry but no room is free today.' Then Joseph said: 'Tonight a child will be born to us, and my wife Mary is so very tired. Is there really nowhere we can stay?' The farmer looked at Mary and saw how beautiful she was and that a wonderful light shone around her, and he remembered the little stable, so he said: 'If you do not mind sharing a stable with my ox you are very welcome to stay there.' He showed them to the stable, gave Joseph a lantern and said, 'Goodnight to you.' Joseph said: 'God bless you,' and closed the stable door.

In the middle of the night it was as if the heavens opened. A great star appeared above the stable and all the angels were singing 'Gloria, Gloria'; and there came from heaven a shining child to be born to Mary, and she called him Jesus.

The Palm Tree and the Well

Long, long ago in a far country where the land was very dry, there was an old broken-down well. Beside it grew a tall, leafy palm tree. Along came a man leading a donkey that was carrying a beautiful woman. They were tired and hungry and very thirsty. The man was Joseph the carpenter and his wife was Mary, and they were travelling to Bethlehem.

When they came to the well, Mary said: 'Please let us rest and have some water to drink.' But Joseph said: 'The well is old and there is no bucket to draw water, and what little water there is, is muddy and dirty.' Then the palm tree shook its branches and one of them fell down to the ground, then it said: 'If you can weave a basket from my leaves, you can draw water.' So Joseph cut the leaves off and Mary wove a basket. And she said: 'A blessing on you kind palm tree and a blessing on the basket that it may never leak.'

Then Joseph said: 'But there is no rope to lower the basket into the well.' And sadly the well said: 'The water is so low, you will never reach it.' Then the palm tree shook down another branch and said: 'Plait my leaves into a rope.' And Mary plaited a long rope and said: 'A blessing on you, good palm tree and a blessing on the rope that it may always be long and strong enough to hold the bucket, and a blessing on the well and its water too.' And when Joseph lowered the bucket into the well, the water sprang up fresh and bubbling and it began to fill up the well once more. The bucket did not leak one drop and Mary and Joseph had lovely fresh water to drink. And the well was happy too, with the water flowing inside it.

After a while, Mary said: 'I am hungry too,' and the palm tree shook down some dates for them to eat and said, 'Take my fruit and eat.' Then Mary blessed the palm tree for the third time and said: 'A blessing on you dear palm tree and may all people learn to live as you do – waving your branches in praise of God and giving your gifts to serve and help mankind.'

And since that day, people make ropes and baskets from the leaves of the palm tree, and everyone enjoys its dates!

The Christmas Story in Verse and Song

'Twas on a deep and silent night,
The earth in darkness lay,
When Mary mild and Joseph
To Bethlehem made their way.

From house to house they wandered
No-one had room for them
'Til at a little farmhouse
They knocked again.

The farmer came and kindly said:
'No room is free today,
But in this little stable here
Gladly you may stay.'

He led them to the stable,
Gave them his lantern light,
And bowed before the maiden
And said, 'Good night.'

And Joseph said, 'God bless you!'
The donkey went, 'Hee-haw!'
The ox went, 'Moo' and bowed his head
And both were munching straw.

And all around the stable
The earth was very quiet,
The whole world seemed to listen
It was the holy night.

Hush, in the silent darkness
I heard an angel's wing,
A golden star from heaven
Came journeying.

It stopped above the stable
To shine with radiance bright,
And there to Mother Mary
Was born the Child of Light.

SILENT NIGHT *can be sung here (while lighting a candle).*

When Joseph saw the child was born
And had no place to rest,
He made Him in the manger
A soft little nest.

And Mary laid Him gently down
And covered His tiny form.
The ox and donkey nestled close
To keep Him warm.

AWAY IN A MANGER *can be sung here:*

Now who was awake
In the night so deep?
Three shepherds were playing
While watching their sheep.

The shepherds grew tired,
Lay down by their sheep,
No sooner they lay
They were fast asleep.
And lo, there appeared a wond'rous light
And angels sang in the holy night... with all their might...

DING DONG MERRILY ON HIGH *can be sung here:*

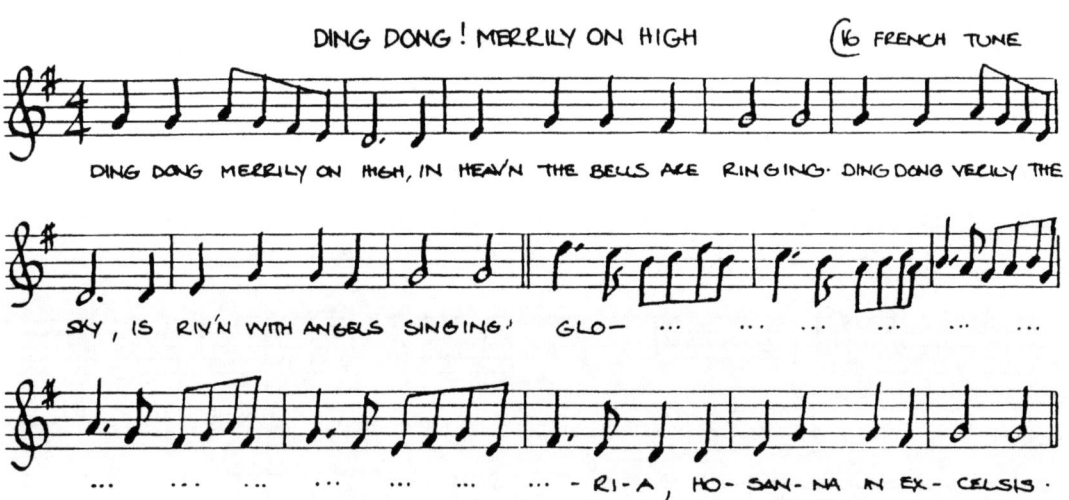

The shepherds awoke and jumped to their feet,
'Come, let us go the child to greet.'
'I'll bring a fur to deck His bed.'
'I'll bring some wool, to rest His head.'
'I'll bring my lamb as white as snow.
Now come, let us go, let us go.'

They came to the stable and knocked at the door
And found baby Jesus on hay and on straw.
Knelt down before the manger low
And gently rocked him to and fro.

And when they had rocked the little child,
They gave their gifts to Mary mild,
And bowed and said 'Goodbye' to all,
And softly left the little stall.

AWAY IN A MANGER *can be sung here (see page 23):*

And the beasts of the field
And the birds of the air
All brought their gifts
To the child so fair

From out of the woods did a cuckoo fly, coo-coo
He came to the manger with joyful cry, coo-coo
He hopped, he curtsied, round he flew,
And loud his jubilation grew, coo-coo, coo-coo, coo-coo.

A pigeon flew over from Galilee, froo-croo,
He strutted and coo'd and was full of glee, froo-croo.
He sang with jewelled wings unfurled
His joy that Christ was in the world.
Froo-croo, froo-croo, froo-croo.

A little rose bush sadly smiled,
Her roses she would give the child,
She could not move, her roots were stuck
Please...who could her roses pluck?

On golden shoes the fairies pranced
And for the child of love they danced,
They brought to Him their roses sweet
And placed them round His tiny feet.

They kissed the little child good-bye.
Then curtsied and away did fly.

Speak the following verse in strong rhythms, stressing each syllable.

Bearded little mountain gnomes
Then came out their mountain homes.

Hammer, hammer, hammer bright
The crystals clear of starry light.

Repeat above while 'hammering' one fist on the other in rhythm

They marched in through the stable door
And laid their gifts upon the floor.
Politely bowed the little gnomes
And went back to their mountain homes.
Their little sacks upon their backs
With clip-a-dee-clap and nick-a-dee nack.

Outside the little stable
From up in heaven high
A little shining golden star
Came twinkling through the sky.
It stopped to stare, then came quite near,
And wondered what was happening there.

The mother with her baby,
Called the light in gaily,
'Come in here, come in here,
Light us with your radiance clear.'

Then all the lights divine,
Brought their golden shine,
And they bowed, deep and low,
Bringing Him their heavenly glow.

TWINKLE, TWINKLE LITTLE STAR *can be sung here*

Three noble kings from far off lands,

Three Magi wond'rous wise,

Were gazing at the stars that night

A'glittering in the skies.

And as they looked a shining star

Appeared in heaven's dome

To lead them to the newborn King

And all three left their homes.

WE THREE KINGS OF ORIENT ARE *can be sung here:*

At last the shining star did rest
Over the stable door,
The three Kings stood there silently
Then knelt down on the floor.

'Greetings to Thee, child so fair,
Gold I bring to Thee.'
'Greetings to Thee, child so rare,
Frankincense I bring to Thee.'
'Greetings to Thee, child so dear,
Healing myrrh I bring to Thee.'

They bowed before the little child
And to His mother Mary mild
Then quietly left the stall.

WE THREE KINGS OF ORIENT ARE *can be sung here (see page 28).*

And the flower bells all rang with joy
Praising the birth of the heavenly boy.

DING DONG MERRILY ON HIGH *can be sung here(see page 24).*

The Little Deaf Girl

A rich man was journeying to Bethlehem with his wife and daughter. The young girl had a delicate, pretty face with big, sad eyes. Her eyes were sad because she could not hear, for she had been deaf from birth. Now sometimes when you cannot hear, you also cannot speak, and so she lived in her own little world, cut off from everything that was going on around her.

All the money her rich father possessed could not help to cure her deafness; and so all that her mother and father could do was to surround little Rachel with their love and care.

They were on their way to Bethlehem and the journey had been long and difficult. Rachel, who rode on a little donkey, was very tired.

Many, many people were walking on the road and there were also many carts and horses and donkeys. Although she could not hear any of the noise, Rachel felt quite dizzy because there was so much going on.

It was getting late and the sun was going down, and everyone had to trot their donkeys quickly in order to be inside the town gates before they were closed. Rachel felt sorry for her donkey and patted it softly on the neck.

Bethlehem was so crowded with travellers that all the inns were full and they could find nowhere to stay. At the other end of town there was a small inn that was also very crowded, but the innkeeper saw that Rachel's father was rich and so he let them have his last small room for lots of money – but there was only room for Rachel under the stairs. Rachel was given a cold damp place where there was a mattress and a blanket and that was all.

After she had eaten with her parents, Rachel was so tired that all she wanted to do was sleep. It did not matter to her if where she slept was hard and uncomfortable. Because she could not hear what people said, she watched their faces and the way they moved. She tried to understand people in her own way and could easily tell how nice or how cruel they were.

The bottom of the stairs was near the front door. The door was open and the innkeeper was speaking to an old man who stood outside. The old man was begging for a place for himself and for his wife to sleep. His young wife stood next to him, holding a donkey by the rein. 'Oh, how beautiful she is,' thought Rachel, and she could not help staring at her. It was as if her heart leapt with joy. There was so much light about the maiden and something so tender and loving streamed from her that the little deaf girl wanted to stay near her, for near this woman she would always feel safe! But the innkeeper had already turned them away. The innkeeper's wife, however, whispered something in the innkeeper's ear so he called them back and said: 'All right, come with me. There is a place in the stable with the animals.' So he took his lantern and led them away from the inn.

With a sigh, Rachel turned back into the room full of chattering people. She signed to her parents that she wanted to sleep and they took her to her little place under the stairs and kissed her goodnight.

While Rachel was thinking of the lovely young woman, she fell asleep. In the middle of the night, when it was still pitch dark around her, she woke up. From her bed she saw the innkeeper standing at the door. He had a burning lantern in his hand, shining on the face of the same old man whom he had taken to the stable.

Rachel could not understand what was going on, but she saw that the lovely young woman was not there and the old man looked very worried. 'Is there something wrong with the lovely woman?' she wondered anxiously. 'Could I perhaps help her?' Suddenly Rachel longed for the young woman. Softly she got up and slipped out of the door, following the old man who was carrying a lantern to light the path. They went to the stable.

It was a poor little stable, just some wooden walls and a roof, but oh my, oh, wonder of wonders! Above the stable shone a star, so bright that Rachel could hardly look at it! When the old man opened the door Rachel saw the wonderful light shining over everything. A beautiful angel stood behind a manger...and in the manger?

As she followed the old man inside, Rachel could not believe her eyes! There, in the manger, lay a tiny newborn child with the face of an angel. The little girl knelt by the mother and laughed with happiness that she was allowed to see something so beautiful. She gazed at the young, glowing mother as if she wanted to say, 'Oh, let me stay here a little. Here I am happy.'

The mother stroked Rachel's dark hair and the baby stretched his little fists out to her. As she reached out her hands to him, and as she held his fists, it was as if her ears suddenly popped! She felt a sharp pain, but when she put her hands over her

ears the pain was already gone. But something wonderful had happened, for as she took her hands away from her ears, she could hear! Yes, she could really hear! At first she could not understand what she was hearing. She heard beautiful music, oh yes, it was the singing of angels that sounded so glorious!

Rachel stayed quite still on her knees beside the manger and listened. She was afraid that if she stood up, the wonder and the glorious sounds would go away.

The old man came to stand beside the manger. Now, for the first time in her life she could hear people talking, although she could not understand the words that they were saying to each other. She understood only with her heart that something wonderful had happened, that she was cured of her deafness and that she had the angel child to thank for it.

Very carefully she stood up. How could she thank the mother and child? She bowed and kissed the seam of the blue cloak which the mother wore. Then she untied the pretty scarf that her father had given her for the journey and gave it to the mother for the child. Smiling, the mother took the soft, warm scarf and spread it over the little child in the manger. Very softly, on tiptoe, Rachel left the stable.

For a long time she thought about the miracle that had happened to her, as she lay in her cold bed under the stairs. She could not sleep again. She waited for the world around her to awaken. Then she heard, for the first time, the crowing of a cock to herald the new day. This new day would also be a new beginning in her life, for now she could hear!

The Story of the Crystal

A long, long time ago, Mother Earth sat deep in her cave under the earth, singing to the little seeds that were sleeping through the winter. Each year it seemed to grow darker within the earth, so she called the little gnomes to her and asked, 'Are you polishing the stones and crystals, for they are losing their light?' The gnomes agreed, for no matter how much they polished the stones, these grew duller and darker.

'We will go and find out why the light is leaving the earth,' said the gnomes; and they chose some beautiful but dull crystals, which they put in their sacks, and with their sacks on their backs they set off on their long journey. For many months they travelled and still they could not find out where the light had gone.

One night, tired and weary, they settled in a field with some sheep. The stars twinkled in the heavens and one, which was bigger and brighter than the others, shone so brightly that the earth was lit as if it were daylight. The gnomes thought that if only they could capture a little bit of the light from that beautiful star it would be enough to make all the stones and crystals shine within the earth, so they set off once again with their sacks on their backs, this time following the great star. As they walked they looked up to see angels flying in the heavens, singing 'Gloria! Gloria!' Their steps quickened and soon they came to a small stable at the back of an inn. From within there came a radiant light spilling out of the doorway. The gnomes stood in the shadows outside, watching.

Some shepherds went in bearing gifts and when they came out again their faces were filled with joy and happiness. 'We have only dull crystals in our sacks,' said the gnomes sadly, 'but we would love to see what this light is that shines so brightly on this dark night.' So quietly they went inside the stable. They saw an ox and an ass standing in the corner, and a father stoking the fire. A mother sat near a manger. She smiled at the gnomes and held out her hand. 'Come closer,' she said, 'come and greet my Son.'

The gnomes took out their dull crystals and held them out to the baby so that He could see the shapes within...and lo...the crystals began to shine and sparkle again, and as they caught the light they sent out rays which filled the air with different colours, and the baby laughed with delight. One gnome turned to the beautiful mother and asked, 'Who is this special child who makes everything shine again?'

And she answered: 'This is the baby Jesus whom God has given to us as a gift, filled with love for the earth and all who live on it. His love will make the earth sing and shine again. Take your crystals back into the earth, little gnomes, with the love which you have felt here tonight, and tell all you see about God's gift to the earth.'

The little gnomes bowed to the mother and the baby and with joy in their hearts and the crystals shining brightly to guide their way, they set off home.

The Animals in the Stable

It was not only the ox and donkey, which were present in the stable at the birth of the Jesus child – a little dove cooed where it slept inside on the beams of the old roof. In the corner sat a fat spider in the middle of her web. A little mouse squeaked in its hole and polished its tiny nose with its paws...

The Ox and the Donkey

Near the manger where the mother had placed her baby, lay the ox and the donkey. From where they lay they could see the baby in the manger surrounded by a halo of light. 'Oh, oh!' brayed the donkey softly to the ox, 'who would have thought that when I brought the maiden here on my back, a little baby would be sleeping in the manger out of which we are supposed to eat. There lies the poor little child in the hay; he should lie in the best and softest cradle in the world with a warm blanket to keep him warm. I would rather have taken him to the finest house in the world, for do you not see how beautiful the child is?'

'Moo,' answered the ox, 'please do not let us eat of the hay, we can go hungry for a while so that the child can have a comfortable bed to lie in. Tomorrow we can eat the grass outside the stable, we will leave the hay to keep the little one warm,' and they settled down and breathed softly over the child to warm the air around Him.

The Doves

The doves on the beams of the stable began to coo, 'I see through the window in the roof that the sky is shining with glorious light and there is movement there too, look, there are flocks of angels flying like birds – oh listen how they are singing, let us join in their song, but quietly, for we do not want to waken the little child.' And the doves cooed gently, a little lullaby for the baby boy.

The Spider

Sitting comfortably in her web, a big fat spider was woken up by the cooing of the doves. Inquisitively she crept out and walked over the beam. Fortunately it was too dark for the doves to see her or she would have been pecked up! Inquisitively she crept quickly to the window for she was curious to see what the doves had been cooing about, and when she saw the angels she called out to them, 'Please give me some of your golden rays so that I can spin a golden thread for the child in the manger.' And lo, when the spider descended from her web she hung on a golden thread, strong and as fine as gossamer. She landed on the hand of Mother Mary and rested happily.

Mary saw the long golden thread and said, 'Thank you good spider, with this beautiful thread I can sew a little vest for my baby,' and the spider was so pleased she climbed slowly the long way back to the web and sat there contentedly.

The Spider's Web

On the other side of the stable sat another spider in its web. Two noisy flies came buzzing in through the window in the roof of the stable. Mary and the baby were fast asleep. 'They will wake the baby,' thought the spider, and as quickly as he could he came down on a strong thread and landed lightly on the side of the manger. He spun and spun as fast as he could, from one side to the other, backwards and forwards, backwards and forwards, until he had spun a fine net over the top of the manger. Now no flies could disturb the little baby from his sleep. When he was finished he quickly climbed his thread back to his web in the corner of the roof.

One of the angels, who was watching over the sleeping baby, gently touched the spider-net and it turned into fine gold.

When Mary woke and saw the beautiful golden net, she wondered where it had come from. She took a stick, which she found in the corner, and gently rolled the fine net onto it and put it away. Every night after that, she unrolled the net over the manger so that no flies would disturb the baby's sleep.

The Mouse

And what was the little mouse doing? When the cooing of the doves awakened it, it looked around in surprise for the stable was full of light. 'What are these strange noises in the manger?' thought the mouse, and went to have a look. It stood on its hind legs and sniffed the strange smells with its sharp little nose. Then it dug its little claws into Mary's blue cloak and climbed into her lap.

Mary was glad that the little mouse was not afraid of her, and she sat still and spoke very softly. 'Dear little mouse, do you want to know who is lying in the manger? It is the little child of God who has been born for the eternal happiness of man and animal, for all of nature, for heaven and earth. Come, I will show you the little child who has been born to bring love to the earth.'

She gently took the little mouse in her hand and held it above the child. The little mouse looked happily into the manger and squeaked, 'Piep – piep, what a beautiful baby, but oh dear, it has not even a warm nest such as I always make for my babies. Oh, if only I knew how to make a warm nest for this wonderful child. It is too cold for him to lie like this and the hay is much too rough for his skin.'

And Mother Mary said, 'Dear little mouse, you have a good and sympathetic heart, and my child will remember your goodness. I will wrap him in a warm blanket, for you are right, it is too cold for him like this'.

Mary put the little mouse carefully on the ground, and it scampered away happily, probably to tell its family all about it.

The Little Glow-Worm

A little beetle overheard the angels telling the shepherds in the field that the holy child was born and lying in the manger, and he was very excited and quickly made his way to the stable. He crawled into the straw of the crib and an angel who was bending over the little child saw him and said, 'What are you doing here, little beetle? Please go to the animals in the field and tell them that a heavenly child has come to the earth.' 'Who will believe me?' asked the little beetle, 'I am so ugly and small.' The angel smiled and stroked the back of the beetle, and as he did so, the beetle began to shine and shine. 'Here, now you carry a light which will show them that you tell the truth,' said the angel.

Full of joy the glow-worm beetle buzzed out of the stable to the hare in the field and deer in the forest. It crawled between stones to the snail and hedgehog. It flew into the trees to the sleeping birds and called all the time: 'A heavenly child has come to the earth, a heavenly child has come to the earth.' In this way the animals learned about the holy child, and the birds were singing long before daybreak!

The Fishes

And who told the fishes?

At the holy hour of midnight, shooting stars fell into all the waters of the world. In this way the fishes learned that it was a special night and the heavenly child had been born on earth; and from that time onwards their scales shone more beautifully than before, and reflected the stars as they swam through the waters of the sea.

The Little Bunnies' Gift

On the night when the baby Jesus was born, two little grey bunnies with white fluffy tails sat outside the stable. They saw the angels flying above the stable singing 'Gloria' to all mankind. They saw shepherds come and go, bearing gifts, they saw such activity from so many other creatures, all trying to see the little baby, that they grew inquisitive. They hopped to the stable door and, when there was a quiet moment, hopped inside and right up to the manger. However, the little bunnies were so small, that even though they hopped as high as they could they could not see over the top of the manger.

'Poor little bunnies,' laughed Mary, watching them jumping around, 'do you also wish to see my son?' She lifted them onto her lap and stroked them gently. The little bunnies looked and looked at the beautiful baby who lay in the manger. They saw the wool on which he lay, and the fur that covered his

tiny form, but his little hands waved in the air, and looked quite cold. 'Poor little one,' thought the bunnies, 'we must give him a gift too.'

Well, do you know, when baby bunnies are born, their mummies love them so much that they take their softest fur from near their hearts and make a soft bed for them to lie in, which keeps them warm and snug. So that is just what they did.

Those little bunnies gave Mary the fur, and when she had thanked each one with a kiss, she fluffed up the fur and rolled it into a little muff to cover her baby's hands and keep them warm. They watched the sleeping baby contentedly, while Mary stroked them some more, then hopped down and out of the stable to tell their children all about it.

The Morning Glory

Near the window of the stable grew a little plant. It too saw the comings and goings from the little stable. It saw the angels flying above, singing 'Gloria' to all mankind, it saw the shepherds bearing gifts, it saw all the animals, outside, but it could not see what was in the stable. 'What is happening inside?' it said to itself, 'it is not fair that I cannot even see where they are taking their gifts, or who to. Oh, how can I see inside?'

A little bunny hopped past. 'Stop,' cried the flower, 'what have you seen?' The bunny sighed with love: 'Something so wonderful, you must see it for yourself!' Oh, that poor little plant was desperate! It looked upwards to the window above, it didn't seem all that high! 'Oh well,' thought the plant, 'I shall have to pull myself up!'

So the little plant started to pull itself up the stable wall. It sent out stickers to help hold onto the wood, and they curled around any little thing which they could grasp. It pulled higher: pull, stick, pull, stick, it went; and at last it reached the window. A little more stretching and into the stable it looked. What a sight met its eyes: a mother sat next to a manger rocking it gently, and in the manger lay a baby, so beautiful that the little plant felt itself growing warm right through, and a beautiful white flower opened at its endmost tip.

Well, the baby lying in the manger had been watching the little plant stretching and pulling, and sending out its stickers to hang on to everything it could, and the baby thought this was really funny and he laughed and laughed; and as he laughed, a little twinkling star flew right out of his eyes and into the heart of the flower where it stuck, twinkling away.

Mary saw what had happened, and went to look at the flower, and as she went up to it her mantle brushed against it and it turned a soft blue, as blue as the blue of her mantle. The little plant shivered with happiness, and slowly climbed around the window, opening beautiful flowers all the time, and soon the window was filled with blue flowers, and in each flower heart twinkled a little star.

And even today you can see these flowers growing over hedgerows and up walls, and if you look into their hearts? Well, go and look for yourself. We call these plants Morning Glory, or Mary's flowers, and now you know why!

The Bird that Sang with the Angels

When the angels began to sing to the shepherds on Christmas night, a little brown bird sang with them, and he sang and sang for joy. He had never sung a note in all his life before, for he was a plain and dull little bird, a real sleepyhead, especially at night. All he had ever thought about was sleeping and eating.

When the angels had gone back into the heavens and the shepherds went down the hillside to see the Christ child, the little bird remembered that he had been singing. He was so surprised that he fell off his perch on a tree into a bed of flowers growing beneath. The flowers had bloomed when the angels sang, even though it was midwinter, so the little brown bird had a soft landing.

'Fly, little bird, fly,' the flowers whispered, 'fly and follow the shepherds.' The little bird did so, and so it happened that he came to the stable and saw the little Christ child lying in the manger. How that little bird loved him! He was so happy that he longed to sing the angels' song again: 'Glory to God in the highest and on earth peace to men of goodwill.'

He wanted to tell all the other little birds that he, a plain little brown bird, had seen the Christ child. 'I'll be the first one to tell them,' he thought as he flew to his tree on the hillside. 'How they will envy me and how important I shall be if I can bring them the good news.'

But while these proud thoughts about himself filled his tiny breast, no song would come from his beak, only tiny harsh noises that disturbed the beauty of the holy night. He tried again and again but he could not sing a note. This amazed him and he even thought to himself: 'It isn't fair, I was the first bird to see the Christ child and really did sing gloriously with the angels, and now I cannot sing at all! The other birds will despise me as much as ever, because I cannot sing.' And while these thoughts filled his breast, he remained unable to sing.

The next morning he flew again to the stable to watch the little Christ child. He found that Mother Mary was trying to hush her little baby to sleep. But the little one was restless, tossing about on his bed of hay, wide awake and almost crying.

Straight away, with love filling his heart for the beautiful baby, the little bird flew to the manger, perched on the side and began to twitter a lovely lullaby. Gently he repeated the words his mother had whispered to him and to his brothers and sisters in their nest when they were baby birds. His mother, too, could not sing, but she used to say softly to her babies over and over again: 'Sleep, little one sleep, hush-a-bye, hush-a-bye, sleep.' And so the little brown bird whispered these same words to the Christ child, thinking only of the restless baby, wanting to help him, pouring love out of his heart towards him. Soon the baby was asleep and the little brown bird flew out into the star-lit night, away to the hillside where the angels had sung.

Now, thinking only of the sleeping Christ child and not of himself at all, he began telling of the happiness in his heart because the little child was sleeping peacefully and Mother Mary had looked so radiant.

Suddenly the plain little brown bird found that he was singing for joy! All through the night he sang praises to the Christ child and presently, all the birds near Bethlehem awoke and listened in wonder to the beautiful music coming from the little plain brown bird. For this was the hour when the bird we know as the nightingale first became a singer.

Robin Redbreast

It was midwinter when the little Christ child was born in the stable, and the night after he was born it was very, very cold even though a small fire had been burning and he was covered with the fur which the shepherds had brought as a gift.

His father, Joseph, went out to search for wood because the fire he had kindled for Mary and the baby was in danger of going out, and he was away longer than he intended because he could not find much wood close to the stable and he had to walk further than he thought.

Mary became anxious because she thought that the little fire might go out before his return. She was worried about the baby for she knew he must be cold, and she

bent over the manger to snuggle him further under the fur. She was just about to go and blow the dying embers of the fire, to try to get it to last a little longer, when suddenly some small brown birds, that had been roosting outside the stable, flew in and made a circle around the dying fire.

They began to fan it with their wings and, as sparks appeared, the remaining twigs and straws caught fire and burned away. Mary threw a last handful of straw onto the glowing embers and the little brown birds hopped closer and beat the air with their wings ever more vigorously. In this way they kept the fire alight until Joseph returned with sticks and logs.

He added the sticks and logs to the fire, and it burned stronger, brighter and much warmer than before.

Mary turned to thank the little birds, and saw that they had scorched their breasts with their efforts to save the fire, and the feathers had burned away and their breasts were hot and red as the flames they had fanned. She called them to her, and as they sat on her hands, completely unafraid, she stroked their breasts gently and said to them: 'Because of the love you have shown my child, from now on you little brown birds shall always have fiery red breasts in memory of your kind deed of keeping the fire alight to warm the baby. People will always love you, and your name from now on will be Robin Redbreast.'

And that is how the robins got their red breasts.

The Nightingale and the Lullaby

A plain little brown bird had built a nest on the beams of the stable. As Mary softly sang a lullaby to the newborn child in the crib, the bird pushed its head over the edge of the nest to listen. It had never heard such a beautiful tune, even from one of its singing brothers.

The little bird hopped onto a beam so that it could listen better to the soft song. But the cold on the journey had made Mary's throat hoarse and soon her singing stopped and she lay down exhausted in a deep sleep. It wasn't long before the little bird heard the child stir restlessly in the crib.

It then lifted its wings and flew softly down onto the edge of the crib. Poor little baby, if only it could sing him to sleep like Mother Mary had. It tried to copy the beautiful singing it had heard from Mary in the hope that the baby would settle down again.

Oh, what a surprise, instead of cheeps and whistles, fine, noble sounds rang out of its throat. It sounded like rejoicing angels from afar, like bells ringing, like the quiet praying of the shepherds, like the gentle moo of the ox. Through this singing Joseph and Mary slept, in spite of the cold night, and the baby in the crib settled down and even smiled in deep sleep because of the wonderful song.

The little brown bird that had copied the song from Mary's lullaby is the nightingale. And do you know, it has never forgotten how to sing it, so that to this day the nightingale sings more beautifully than any other bird in the whole world.

The Shepherds' Verse

See the shepherds go to sleep
On the hillside, by their sheep.
In the quiet starry air
Angel song is everywhere.

The Shepherds' Star

Many, many years ago, at the time of the very first Christmas, a little shepherd boy called John was looking after his lambs.

One evening as he was resting by the fire, he heard a mother sheep bleating. When John went to look he found that she was bleating because her little lamb was lost. The older shepherds said to John: 'Go and find your lamb and we will watch the flock of sheep together and wait for you.'

John walked into the night. The light of the stars lit his way and so did the moon that shone brightly in the heavens. He walked for a long, long time until he came to the edge of a high mountain cliff. John could go no further and, exhausted, he sat down in despair and looked around wondering what he should do next. Then he saw a golden stairway that stretched up, up, up, towards the moon. John began to climb the stairway, and with each step his legs became stronger and stronger so that he was no longer tired. Upwards he went until he was amongst the stars.

There, in a beautiful garden, sat a maiden. She wore a red dress, and a blue mantle covered her like a cloak, and stars sparkled in her hair. At her feet stood John's little lamb. The maiden was combing his fluffy fleece and weaving the wool from the comb into a little shirt. This woolly shirt shone with light from the sun and the moon and the stars.

The beautiful maiden smiled at him and said: 'John, your little lamb kindly came to offer his wool to make this little shirt warm for my coming child. Now it is finished and I am grateful for his gift. Please take him back to his mother on the earth for I can hear her calling him. She must wonder where he is.'

The young shepherd gathered the little lamb in his arms and said: 'Please, before I leave this heavenly place, may I see this child who will wear such a beautiful shirt? For he must be very special.'

'Soon he will be born in the town of Bethlehem. Come and see him there,' said the beautiful maiden. 'But Bethlehem is so far away,' said John, 'it is winter and the world is dark. I fear I shall lose my way.'

The maiden pointed to a star, bigger and brighter than all those around him, and said: 'See this star, it is the one which will bring the heavenly shining child to the earth. If you follow this star then you will find your way to the place where He will be born.' John thanked the beautiful maiden and said goodbye to her. He carried his lamb back to the flock where its mother bleated with happiness to see it. John told the other shepherds all about his journey, and about the maiden who wove the special shirt for her child.

The next night while the shepherds were sleeping in the fields, a great shining star shone brightly in the heavens. John dreamed he could hear beautiful singing: 'Gloria, Gloria'. He opened his eyes and looked up to see the radiant star. All around it angels were singing and bells were ringing. 'Come,' said John to the other shepherds, 'we must follow that star to Bethlehem where we will find the new-born child who will bring love and light to the earth.'

So each shepherd took a gift for the child. One took some fur to deck His bed, another took some wool to rest His head, and John took his lamb as white as snow, and they followed the star to Bethlehem.

In a little stable they found the child of light, and gave their gifts to his mother Mary, who wore a mantle as blue as the heavens. They knelt before the little manger where the child lay, and saw that truly he was the most beautiful child in the entire world.

The Shepherd Boy and the Lamb

A little shepherd boy lay sleeping with the shepherds in the field one night. The fire warmed them and the sparks from the flames flew up into the night sky like the stars shining so brightly in the heavens. As he lay sleeping he dreamed that he heard bells ringing and angels singing and he awoke with a start. The fire had died down and all was quiet, except for the occasional bleating of the sheep as they settled down to sleep. The little shepherd cuddled close to his little lamb, nestling into the warm wool and went back to sleep.

In the morning when he awoke, he went with his lamb to the stream to drink and wash his face. When he had washed he found that his lamb had disappeared. 'Lambie, Lambie where are you?' called the shepherd boy, and he began to search everywhere for him, running down the stream, over the fields, through bushes and grass, until he came to a forest. 'He must have gone in here,' he said and wandered further and further into the forest and away from the other shepherds, still calling his lamb.

Before he knew what had happened he felt himself falling...crashing through leaves and branches until he landed with a bump on the ground at the bottom of a hole. He jumped up, and, relieved to find he wasn't hurt he brushed himself off, but no matter how hard he tried to climb out of the hole he couldn't find a way up, so he sat down on a root and began to cry. Suddenly he heard a tinkling sound. 'Lambie, is that you?' he called, and the little lamb's furry face appeared above the hole. 'Please go back to the field and fetch the shepherds to help me out of this hole,' he cried. The lamb went bouncing off, the bell tinkling softer and softer as he went further and further away.

The sun went down and the stars appeared through the trees, burning so brightly in the heavens that it was like daylight shining into his deep hole. Suddenly he did not feel afraid, and as the shepherd boy watched the stars, he heard the sound of bells ringing. It was as if the whole of the heavens was filled with music...'ding dong merrily on high, in heaven the bells are ringing...Gloria...' he sang loudly, joining in with the heavenly singing.

Suddenly the bells became louder and louder, and he looked up to see his lamb, the sheep and the shepherds, looking down at him. His lamb had fetched them after all! They pulled him up out of the deep hole and, wrapping him in fur to keep him warm, they carried him back to the fire, his lamb running happily behind him.

'Did you hear the heavenly bells ringing, the angels singing, and why are the stars shining so brightly?' asked the boy. The old shepherd answered, 'Tonight is special, for a heavenly shining child has been born to bring joy and love to the earth. When we have had some food and drink, we will go to find him; the angels have told us to follow that bright star you can see over there.'

So they ate and drank by the fire. And before they set off to follow the star, the old shepherd gave the little boy a gift too...a little bell to hang around his neck. 'Here,' he said, 'now you will not get lost again, for wherever you go we will hear your little bell ringing, and we will find you, just as your little lamb found you tonight.'

The little shepherd boy thanked the shepherd, and each shepherd took a gift for the child. One took some fur to deck His bed, another took some wool to rest His head, and the little shepherd took his lamb as white as snow. As they walked over the fields following the bright star, he could hear his little golden bell tinkling as brightly and sweetly as the bells ringing in the heavens.

And in a little stable they found the Child of Light, and gave their gifts to his mother Mary, who wore a mantle as blue as the heavens. They knelt before the little manger where the child lay, and saw that truly he was the most beautiful child in all the world.

And the air was full of the sound of angels singing 'Gloria' to all mankind.

The Good Shepherds

Long, long ago in a land called Judea, there lived three poor shepherds. Every morning they were up early and took their sheep out of the stall to the fields. One day a big fire burned the land, so when the shepherds took their sheep to the field there was not one green blade of grass left and the field was black and dry. The poor sheep ran around bleating and did not find a single branch to nibble, so the three shepherds had to take their sheep to a field much further away from the burnt place.

The youngest shepherd stayed behind to look after the last of the sheep and drive them on. Suddenly he thought he heard someone crying. He stood still and looked around but he saw no one. Then he heard a soft voice but he could not work out where it was coming from for there was no one to be seen. He listened very carefully; and it seemed as if the voice came from a little burnt rose bush that stood nearby. He bent over the plant and heard her say quite clearly: 'Oh shepherd please help me, for although my leaves may be burnt, my roots are still living.'

The young shepherd knelt down, loosened the soil near her roots, and poured water from his flask around them. 'Thank you very much good shepherd, now I can live again.' She then pushed one sweet rose out of her stem between the burnt leaves. The shepherd boy picked the rose, thanked the little rose bush and walked on.

Far in the distance, the shepherd saw the other shepherds walking with the sheep and he ran as fast as he could to catch up with them. At last they came to a place where no fire had been and where sweet grass and lovely herbs grew. The sheep were very happy and ate greedily.

The second shepherd threw his cloak on the ground and lay down with his arms under his head and looked at the blue sky. Suddenly he thought he heard soft crying. He sat up and looked around. He could only see sheep nearby so what could it be? He sat very still and listened carefully, and he heard again a sniffling and crying. Was it a mouse? The sound came from inside a little bush. He carefully pushed the branches aside and there sat a rabbit holding up its little paw, which had drops of blood dripping from it. 'Oh, good shepherd, help me,' it pleaded. The shepherd knelt down by the hurt rabbit and carefully took the little paw and washed it well with water from his water-flask until it was clean. He then took a little pot of fat and smeared it over the paw and bound his handkerchief around it. He gave the rabbit some water to drink from his bottle and stroked its little head. Thankfully the rabbit licked the shepherd's hand and said: 'Thank you very much good shepherd, now I can walk again.' And it jumped away on all four paws.

The shepherd stood up and saw that his sheep were far away, so he grabbed his cloak and ran as fast as he could to be with the other shepherds.

It was now midday and the sun was very warm. The shepherds had come with their sheep to a far place. The sheep were tired of walking and wanted to rest. The oldest shepherd followed behind, herding the last sheep into the field to be with the others.

He thought he heard soft calling so he stood still and looked around. Nearby he saw a little hut. It had a crooked door and some of the roof was broken. Was there someone living inside who needed help? Quickly the old shepherd went there. He opened the creaking door and looked inside.

On a bed lay an old woman, and when she saw the shepherd come in she said softly: 'Ah, good man, help me please for I am sick.' The shepherd went to her side and said: 'Of course I will help you dear mother, but let me go and tell my friends that I will come to them later.'

It wasn't long before he returned. First he made a warm fire in the fireplace so that the old lady could get warm. Then he cooked some porridge for her to eat. He cleaned the house and fetched water and firewood. After a while the old lady sat up in her bed and called out: 'I feel so much better now, I believe that tomorrow I will be able to get up again. Thank you very much, good shepherd, for your help.'

When the shepherd returned to his friends and to his sheep, it was getting dark and the stars were beginning to shine in the sky. The shepherd said: 'It is too late to take our sheep back to their stalls. Let us spend the night with our sheep in the open field.'

The three shepherds made a little fire to warm themselves and cooked something to eat. 'We are tired from the long day. Look how well our sheep are sleeping, so now we can also close our eyes and sleep here too.'

They each chose a good place to sleep and lay down. In the night, while they slept under the beautiful starry sky, the shepherds awoke. It seemed to them as if all the stars in heaven were becoming brighter and brighter, and a great shining star appeared as if calling them to follow. The heavens were filled with angels singing 'Glory to God in the highest, and peace on earth to men of goodwill.'

Yes, the shepherds followed the star to Bethlehem, and what did they see there? Well, that is another story.

The Torch

At the time the little Jesus child was about to be born, there lived an old shepherd named Gaul. On the night when the shepherds were lying in the fields and the angels brought their message, Gaul was not with them. He was also not with them when the shepherds went to look for the stable where the child was born.

The old shepherd was watching over his grandson who was lying ill in bed. He had been ill for some days and this night the old man was very worried about him for he seemed to be getting worse. Sadly he looked at the little boy as he tossed to and fro restlessly. He was weak and crying softly, and his eyes were burning with fever. The old man longed to say something to the child but found that he could not speak. The mother also sat by the bed holding her child's hand.

The old shepherd went to the door in order to take deep breaths of the fresh evening air, then he stepped outside into the quiet night.

He thought: 'Perhaps I shall find some peace here,' and looked up to the glittering stars. He saw a wonderful light in the night sky, but could not make out where it was coming from.

'This is strange,' he thought, and, as if in a dream, he walked into the fields where he knew his friends the other shepherds were watching over the sheep. They were sleeping peacefully, but so also were the dogs that should have been keeping watch over them. It looked as if all danger from wolves had been forgotten. Did they feel so safe on this strange night?

'Something wonderful is happening,' thought Gaul, 'but I can't make out what it is.' He looked around again and stared at the sky. Then he saw where the shining light was coming from.

In the night sky shone a large bright star which he had never seen before. It was so brilliant that its wonderful light spread all around him. Filled with wonder, the old shepherd gazed at the star, which was nearer than he had first thought, for it moved before him and lit the path which led to Bethlehem.

The star beckoned him to follow and moved further on before him. He no longer felt worried and sad but followed the star joyfully and at peace.

It was very quiet and still around him. No leaf stirred on the trees, no animal called fearfully in the peaceful night and no birds flew startled out of the branches of the trees.

The star moved on and the shepherd followed it until it came to a stop above a stable near to the town of Bethlehem. Gaul went softly to the stable and listened carefully.

He heard many different noises coming from inside. The 'moo' of a cow, the 'hee-haw' of a donkey, the clear voices of a man and a woman; and he thought he heard the cry of a very small baby.

He opened the door slightly and looked inside. What he saw was of great wonder and beauty. Bathed in glowing, pure light sat a young woman cradling her newborn child in her arms. All around were angels, singing 'Gloria'.

Taking his cap off his grey head, he stepped inside and knelt down. The mother smiled and held the baby nearer to him so that he could see it better. With great tenderness, the old man stroked the little fist that the baby held out to him. He whispered loving words to it, which came straight from his heart.

'Oh, dear little one,' he whispered, 'are you our long expected child from heaven? Are you a king, and yet born in a stable? What can I give to you, little king? I kneel before you with empty hands.'

The child looked at him with shining eyes and Gaul suddenly thought of his grandson, who was sick in bed. Yet now he was no longer worried for his heart was full of joy. Tears of happiness streamed down his wrinkled cheeks and turned into pearls as they dropped onto his folded hands. Even this did not surprise Gaul for so many wonderful things had happened this night. Gratefully he gathered up the pearls and gave them to the young mother as a gift for the little child.

Near to Gaul stood an old lantern. Joseph, the baby's father, wanted to light the lantern in order to go to the inn, for he wished to ask for a soft blanket for the mother and child. When the old shepherd saw that Joseph had difficulty lighting his lantern, he lit a twig and with this flame lit the lantern. Joseph thanked him and left the stable.

The old shepherd stood with the burning twig in his hand. As he looked at the little flame he thought: 'Perhaps I should take some of this light to my own hut? For surely this small flame is part of the divine light that is shining here, and will bring comfort to our sick child.'

The old man knelt down and made a small fire of dried twigs and straw. Then he found a stout strong stick and an old rag. He tied the rag around one end of the stick and dipped it in oil. In this way he made a torch and lit it with his small flame. He said goodbye to the mother and child, left the stable softly and walked across the fields, taking the shortest way home to his hut.

The wind made the flame of his torch flicker and he walked as fast as his old legs would carry him. When he reached his hut he stopped before going in. He had stayed away so long, what would his daughter think of him? And what if the child had died? Then that wonderful feeling of joy and peace streamed into him again, and with a happy smile on his old face he stepped into the hut.

His daughter was kneeling at the foot of the little boy's bed and she looked up, startled when her father came in with his flaming torch. When she saw the joy and happiness in his eyes, she kept still and looked at him, wondering what he would do next.

With the burning torch in his hand, the old man stood in front of the bed. With big surprised eyes the little boy looked at the light which filled the room with a radiant glow. The dancing flames excited him and yet gave him rest. Fear vanished from his thin little face and his mouth opened with amazement as the old shepherd sat next to the bed and softly told them of all the wonderful things that he had been allowed to see.

After a while, the little boy lay quite still and gazed at the last flickering flames of the torch, which was now nearly out. It had made him sleepy, as had the beautiful story that his grandfather had told him. The pain in his head had gone. He could not keep his eyes open, his breathing became peaceful and quiet, and he slept. His mother tucked him in carefully so that he would not get cold.

The old man and his daughter knelt by the bed and gave thanks for the miracle, for they knew that the little boy was now cured of his illness and was well again.

How the Rose Lost its Petals

A long, long time ago, near the little town of Bethlehem, there lived a young boy whose name was Benjamin. Benjamin's father was a shepherd, but Benjamin was too young to look after sheep and so his father gave him only one little lamb of his own to look after.

Now Benjamin loved his little lamb more than anything in the whole world, well, almost more than anything, because he also loved his beautiful pink rose. It had 15 petals and grew just outside his bedroom window. Every morning he would go into the garden, look up at the sky and say:

Father Sun, shine on my rose, but not too hot,
Sister Rain, rain on my rose, but not too wet,
Brother Wind, blow on my rose, but not too hard.

Every evening he would look out of his window at the stars and say:

Sister Moon and every twinkling star,
Shine on my rose and give her good dreams.

Benjamin worked hard in his garden, hoeing and raking, weeding and watering until it looked spick and span so that every flower bloomed and there was not a weed to be seen.

Benjamin also loved to play hide-and-seek with his little lamb. One day, when it was his little lamb's turn to hide and Benjamin had his eyes closed, the little lamb found that the gate was left open and ran as fast as he could out of the gate and over the fields. When Benjamin went to look for him he hunted high and low and could not find him anywhere; then he noticed that the gate was open and there, far, far away, he could see his little lamb running as fast as his little legs could move.

Benjamin called and called but his little lamb was too far away to hear. He burst into tears: 'Little lamb, come back, come back,' he sobbed. Just then he heard a beautiful voice singing:

Benjamin, please dry your eyes,
Now is not the time to cry,
All mankind rejoices this morn,
For the Christ child has been born.

Benjamin couldn't believe his eyes for there, in front of him, stood a shining angel. 'The Christ child?' he asked. 'Where? May I see Him?' The angel answered:

In Bethlehem, in stable low,
Tween ox and ass, there you may go.

'What about my little lamb?' asked Benjamin. And the angel answered, singing:

I will find him where he roams
And will straightway send him home.

'I must take something very precious to give to this little child,' thought Benjamin. 'I know, I will take him my rose.'

He went to his rose: 'Come, my rose,' he said, 'you are coming with me to Bethlehem.' He carefully cut the stem, and holding his rose, which had 15 petals, off he went.

Bethlehem was a full day's journey away and, after walking for a long while, Benjamin became tired and thought that he would have a rest, so he put his rose carefully down and sat on the grass under a shady tree. After a while along came a spider and sat next to him. Benjamin didn't like spiders so he stood up and stamped on it. Then he picked up his rose...but it looked different. He counted the petals: '1,2,3,4,5,6,7,8,9...10! Ten petals! How could that be? I'm sure that I counted 15,' thought Benjamin. So, taking his rose, which now had only 10 petals, he set off for Bethlehem.

Benjamin walked and walked for a long time and at last he came to a well. He was very thirsty so he put his rose down and bent over the well, scooping up the water in his hands in order to drink. While he was drinking he saw a dog coming towards him. 'Are you also thirsty?' asked Benjamin. The dog barked and wagged its tail. 'Go away, I'm drinking first,' said Benjamin, but the dog would not go and started to whine. Benjamin became cross and smacked it on the nose, and the poor dog ran away yelping.

When he had finished drinking he picked up his rose...but what was this? 1,2,3,4...5 petals...? Oh dear! Benjamin did not know what to do. Should he go home? Should he go on? 'Oh well,' he thought, 'I might as well go on.' So, taking his rose, which now had only 5 petals, Benjamin walked further until he came to a little hill outside the gates of Bethlehem.

As there was still time before the gates closed, Benjamin sat down to watch all the people coming and going through the gates. He saw an old woman walking on the road towards him. She was carrying a heavy bundle. 'Poor old woman,' he thought, 'she looks so tired.'

'Please help me carry this bundle home,' the old woman asked Benjamin, 'I don't live far from here.' 'I'm sorry,' answered Benjamin, 'I haven't the time,' and he went on sitting while the old lady went on her way.

When it was time to go he picked up his rose...but...oh dear, only 1...no...2 petals? What happened? How could that be? And how could he take the rose to the baby when it had only 2 petals? Again, Benjamin did not know what to do.

Perhaps he would just look through the window! So, taking his rose, which now had only 2 petals, Benjamin walked through the town of Bethlehem and at last came to the stable. He softly crept to the door and peered inside.

A wonderful light seemed to shine around the head of a maiden, who was bending over a manger. She was the most beautiful lady he had ever seen. Just then she lifted her head and saw him, then she smiled, and came outside to greet him and ask his name. Benjamin quickly hid his rose behind his back.

'What do you have behind your back, Benjamin?' she asked. 'A rose,' he answered, 'at least it was a rose, but it isn't a rose anymore.' 'How do you mean it isn't a rose anymore?' asked Mother Mary. 'Well, it lost all its petals,' he said. 'Why did it lose its petals, Benjamin?' she asked. 'I don't know,' he whispered, and he was so ashamed that he didn't know where to look and hung his head.

'When did it lose its petals?' she asked. Benjamin thought back. 'Well, the first time was when I stamped on the spider, and...the second time was when I hit the dog, and...the third time was when I didn't help the old lady.' 'And so?' asked Mother Mary, 'what does that tell you?'

'Oh dear,' said Benjamin, 'I shouldn't have killed the spider, because he was also one of God's creatures, and...and...I shouldn't have hit the dog for he was also thirsty. And I could have helped the old lady. Oh, I am so sorry...and so ashamed!' Tears ran down his cheeks and he wished that the ground would open up and swallow him.

Mother Mary put her arms around him and he felt all warm and cosy. 'If you are truly sorry then give me the rose,' she said. 'But it has only 2 petals!' he cried. 'Give it to me and come,' she told him.

Benjamin followed her into the stable. He came to the manger and looked into the crib. Oh wonder of wonders, what a beautiful child! Mother Mary placed the rose with its 2 petals into the crib and the baby touched it with His little dimpled hands and Benjamin could not believe his eyes, for lo and behold, there were 15 petals again! And the rose was shining and glowing with the same light that surrounded the baby.

Mother Mary took the rose, gave it to Benjamin and said: 'This rose will never die. Take it home with you, and when you look at it always think about how it lost its petals, but even more important, think about how it got its petals back again.'

Benjamin was so happy that he did not know what to say. 'Thank you, Mother Mary, thank you dear little baby, thank you, thank you.' Then Benjamin, with a heart filled with love and joy at what he had seen, slowly turned and went home to his little lamb who was waiting patiently for him.

From that day onwards he never ever forgot how the rose lost its petals and how it got its petals back again.

Well, that rose has never died, and if we can find our way to where it is, we will still see it there as beautiful and fresh as ever.

How Joseph Lit his Torch

A long, long time ago, in mid-winter, an old man called Joseph went out on a dark night to look for some live coals in order to kindle a fire, for he wanted to warm the stable where his wife had just given birth to a baby. He went from house to house and knocked at each door, but no one answered for it was late and most of the people were asleep.

Joseph walked on and on until he had left the village behind, and came out into the open country where the fields stretched before him. At last, a long way off, he saw the gleam of a fire. As he walked towards it he saw that the fire was alight in an open field where many sheep slept peacefully, huddled closely together around the fire. An old shepherd, wrapped in a thick cloak, sat on a rock and watched over the flock. As the man came nearer he saw that three big dogs were asleep at the shepherd's feet.

All three dogs woke up when they heard him coming. They opened their big mouths as though they were going to bark, but there was no sound. They jumped up and made as if to jump at Joseph, but they could do him no harm. The shepherd seemed almost asleep, and all the sheep were fast asleep, lying so close together that Joseph wondered how he could reach the shepherd to speak to him. He decided to make his way through as best he could; so, very gently, he wove his way in and out among the sleeping animals, and not one moved or woke up.

When Joseph had almost reached the fire the shepherd looked up. He was a bad-tempered old man, unfriendly and stern to other human beings. Joseph went right up to the cross old man and said: 'Good friend, please help me, my wife has just given birth to a child, and we have no fuel for a fire. I must make a fire to warm her and the little one.'

At first the shepherd only stared, for he wanted to say 'No', but when he saw that the dogs did not bite, and that the sheep did not stir as the man stepped over them, he said in a gruff voice: 'Yes, take what you need.' But he thought to himself: 'Surely this man cannot pick up burning coals?'

To the shepherd's amazement Joseph bent down and picked up the burning coals with his bare hands and was not even burned! He wrapped the coals in his cloak and it wasn't even scorched, and he carried the coals as easily as if they were apples or nuts. Joseph thanked the shepherd warmly, and just as he was moving away the shepherd called him back. 'What kind of night is this,' he said, 'when dogs don't bite, and the sheep are not frightened, and the fire does you no harm?'

Joseph was eager to get back to his wife, but he stood still for a moment and said gravely: 'I cannot tell you for I believe you must see it for yourself! Good night, God bless you and many, many thanks.'

Now the shepherd was so bewildered at these happenings that he left the dogs to guard his sheep and followed Joseph at a distance to see if he could discover his secret. He followed him through the sleeping village and out the other side, where he saw the man going into a little stable.

The old shepherd quietly entered the stable and saw the mother lying on the straw with her little baby in her arms. Something warm and kind stirred in his heart and he wanted to help. 'Oh, that beautiful child must not freeze,' he thought, so he opened his leather knapsack and took out a soft white sheepskin and handed it to the father. 'Take it,' he said, 'and wrap the child up or he will freeze on this cold night.'

And the moment his heart melted with compassion, his eyes were opened. He saw great light shining around the three figures in the stable, and hosts of angels were singing that on this night was born the Saviour who is Christ the Lord.

The shepherd was so happy that he fell down on his knees and through his tears he saw the child who had been sent from God to bring peace on earth to all mankind.

The Wise Men's Verse

Star high, baby low,
'Twixt the two, wise men go.
Find the baby, grasp the star,
King of all things near and far

The Three Kings

There was once a beautiful castle in which a king lived. His name was King Melchior, and he was as kind as he was good. One night he decided to go up into the tallest tower of his castle so that he could look at the stars, which seemed to be shining more brightly than ever. He took with him a golden cup, for when he looked into this cup he could see pictures of the stars reflected.

That night he held his cup in such a way that he saw the stars, and the stars formed a crown…a crown around the head of a mother. She wore a cloak as blue as the heavens and held a child on her knee. And as the kind King Melchior looked into his cup, he saw that she beckoned to him, and he knew that he must go to her. 'But how will I find you?' he asked, and as the picture of the mother faded from the cup a great shining star appeared, and he looked up to see it shining in the heavens, and knew that he must follow that star.

Melchior called his men to bring the camels, and he put on his gold crown and his red cloak. In his hands he held a box carrying only the finest gold to take to the little child who had been born. And so kind King Melchior set out across the desert, following the star.

In another country far, far away lived another king, wise King Balthazar. In his castle he had a grand hall with a most wonderful ceiling. This ceiling could roll back and open the room to the stars. King Balthazar loved to sit in his hall with the ceiling rolled back, and watch the smoke from the frankincense curl upwards and drift out of the roof towards the stars. Often he could see pictures in the smoke from the sweet-smelling herb.

One night he rolled back the ceiling, and the stars shone more brightly and beautifully than before. As he looked at the smoke from the sweet-smelling frankincense drifting towards the stars, he saw in the smoke a mother with a cloak as blue as the heavens. A shining crown of stars twinkled in her hair, and on her knee a child beckoned to him. 'How will I find you?' asked King Balthazar. 'Follow the star,' said the mother, and the picture faded. As he looked up, he saw a star shining so brightly in the heavens that he knew it must be the one he must follow.

Wise King Balthazar brought a jewelled box filled with frankincense, put on his beautiful blue cloak, called his men to bring the horses and rode over the fields to follow the star.

In another land lived a king called Caspar. In the gardens of his palace was a deep well, in the waters of which he could see the stars reflected. But in his country it had not rained in a long, long time and there was so little water that the only plants that grew were in his garden, and they were bushes of myrrh. People came from all around, for when they had been hurt or were in pain, the good king Caspar made an ointment from the bushes of myrrh which could heal them.

Each night he knelt by the well (for it was the only one with water still left in it) and prayed for rain to come. One night as he knelt by the well, he saw stars reflected in the water. They shone so brightly that they dazzled his eyes, and from the middle of the stars emerged the picture of a mother with a cloak as blue as the heavens, and a crown of stars around her head. On her knees sat a child who beckoned to him. 'How do I find you?' he asked, and the mother pointed to a star which shone brighter than all the others, and he knew he must follow that star. All of a sudden drops began to fall into the well, the picture of the mother disappeared and the rain fell, watering the parched earth. King Caspar knew that his prayers had been answered. The old king put branches of the healing myrrh into a box, put on his green cloak, and set off on his journey, always following the star.

For many days the three kings travelled until they met in the desert, and then all three together followed the star until it stopped above a stable. In the stable sat a mother with a child on her knee, and her cloak was as blue as the heavens, and in her hair was a crown of stars. Around the child light glowed and the kings knew that He must be the newborn king. They took off their crowns before Him, and knelt down on the floor.

'Greetings to thee, child so fair, gold I bring to thee,' said the good King Melchior. 'Greeting to thee, child so rare, frankincense I bring to thee,' said the kind King Balthazar. 'Greetings to thee, child so dear, healing myrrh I bring to thee,' said the wise King Caspar. They bowed before the little child, and gave their gifts to his mother who thanked them graciously. The child raised His hand and smiled gently at the three kings, who quietly left the stall.

As they left the stable they marvelled at all they had seen, and that such a child who had been born in a stable could be king of all mankind, bringing joy and love to the world.

The Wise Men's Well

Once upon a time, three wise men from the East were following a wandering star to pay homage to the newborn King, the Jesus child, who had been born to bring light and love to the earth. They prepared gifts, organised camels, horses and servants to follow them, and departed their kingdoms.

King Melchior brought a casket of gold. King Balthazar carried sweet-smelling frankincense, and King Caspar bore a jar of the healing herb myrrh.

Each king was wonderfully arrayed in robes of red, green and midnight blue, and brought with them pearls and precious stones.

The star went before them but, after following it for many weeks, their rich trappings that had so delighted them when they left became a burden. Often they feared for their riches, or that they might be robbed, or even that the swirling sands of the desert would swallow them up. They no longer saw the wind as a friend, sifting and rustling through the grasses, but as an enemy, scratching their skins and blowing sand in their eyes. But they walked ever onwards, led by the star that hung brightly in the heaven.

They grew tired, and began to wonder, 'What if there is no child?' 'What if the star is going nowhere?' They began to doubt their vision, that of the mother with a crown of stars in her hair, and the child on her lap beckoning to them. Did they dream it all?

Soon they came to an arid desert where no trees grew, and no grasses swayed in the wind. They journeyed on, and it wasn't long before they found their water growing scarce, and there was no more anywhere. They slept in snatches, journeying on through the night when it was cooler and the star shone brighter than ever before them. More and more they doubted if they were really doing the right thing.

One evening, however, when the sun disappeared behind the sand dunes, and it grew dark, no star appeared to greet them. The kings cried to their God in anguish: 'Forgive us, we doubted the child, we are lost...lost. No crowns or rich robes can help us now.' The kings wandered in the desert without the star to guide their way, until in the dawn's first light they chanced on a green place among the sand dunes where palm trees stood – an oasis! The kings hurried towards it and stooped to drink from the well that stood at the centre, when lo, they saw reflected in the depths of the well their star shining brightly! And even as they gazed at it in wonder, it changed to the picture that they had all seen before. There, in the depths of the blue water, they saw a mother with a crown of stars in her hair, and on her knee sat the shining child, beckoning them to come to Him. The wise men lifted their heads and looked into the heavens...and there was the star, shining brightly even in the midst of the day. They filled their water flasks and jugs, drank their fill, and journeyed on rejoicing, sure now that they would find the child.

As the years passed by, drought crept ever nearer that oasis where the well stood under the palm trees. The sands of the desert blew, the sun shone brightly in the heavens, and not a drop of rain fell. Slowly, inch by inch, the water in the well began to dry up, the palm trees died, the green grass disappeared, and travellers could hardly find a drop to drink, and had to go onwards through the desert, ever searching for more water. At last there was nothing left but a dry well, shrivelled grass and dead trees.

One day, a procession appeared on the horizon – camels, horses, servants and tent bearers – causing the sand to fly up in small dust clouds as they came closer and closer to the dried-up place where the oasis had been. In the front of the procession walked the three wise men. They arrived at the well and looked into its dried-up depths where no water remained, just a few stones at the bottom. Then they called their servants to them.

The servants came carrying pitchers of water, which they poured into the well. Then the wise men said: 'Because you restored hope to us, and showed us the newborn King in your waters, and because you quenched our thirst with revelation of the child, we bless you with water from paradise which no drought can ever dry up.' And the water bubbled to the top of the well, clear and fresh and clean.

From that day the well never dried up, no matter how harsh the drought, no matter how bright the sun, no matter how scarce the rain. The palm trees once again grew and bore ripe dates, the grass and reeds swayed green in the breeze, and people who came to that oasis were always provided with fresh water from the well.

And to this day they call that well 'The Wise Men's Well' and it always blesses those who drink from it.

The Camel

Far away in eastern lands, there lived a rich and mighty king. He was also a wise and good man. He studied books and he also studied the stars and the signs in the sky.

Besides the palace there were stables, just as magnificent as the palace. They were built of shining marble, and inside, the stalls and stables were of polished hardwoods, and the water troughs of solid brass. There were not only fine horses in these stables, for in this country people also rode camels, and the king, of course, kept camels in his stable, or rather his servants kept them, for he had a great many servants.

Now the camel is a proud animal. He is not handsome or particularly well mannered. He has thick sneering lips and he spits when he is cross, and even the camel of a poor man is proud and haughty. So you can imagine how grand were the camels of this king. A camel, for all his pride, has to kneel down on the ground in order for a rider to mount him, and in the king's stable there was one camel who was so very proud that he would only kneel for the king to ride him, and for no one else.

One morning there was a great deal of bustle and excitement in the king's stable. The camels could clearly see that preparations were being made for a journey. Others were being saddled ready for riding. Of course the camels were not too proud to listen to the servants' conversations as they worked. It seemed that last night something very important had happened. A new star had appeared in the sky, the brightest ever seen, and the ancient books of the wise king told him that this was the sign that the greatest King in all the world was born, one who was wiser and mightier than any other. Now they were preparing for a journey, to find him.

When all was ready, the king mounted his very proud camel. He carried with him a beautiful casket containing the precious gift he had chosen to take to the newborn King. The very proud camel liked the idea of this journey. They must be going somewhere very grand if they were going to visit such a great King! The proud camel looked forward to seeing a magnificent palace or castle. He wondered what splendid stables there might be. It seemed that this new great King was only a baby, but if he were as important as the slaves had said, no doubt everything would be very royal indeed.

It was a long journey, but at last it seemed the day had come when they would arrive. The very proud camel began to look ahead, waiting for some grand castle

to appear. They came to a small town, which certainly didn't look very grand, and there, to the camel's surprise, he had to pick his way through narrow dirty streets. He was astonished when they stopped outside a little shabby old inn, with a tiny tumbledown stable beside it. Surely this could not be anything to do with the king whom they had come to find?

But here he was ordered to kneel in the dirt ready for his master to dismount. And now his master was taking his precious gift into this scruffy place! The camel could hardly believe his eyes. Outside the tumbledown stable was tethered a donkey. Normally the camel was much too proud to talk to a donkey, but he was so surprised at what was going on today that he forgot himself and asked: 'Who lives in this place?'

'Mary and Joseph are staying here, with the new baby, little Lord Jesus,' said the donkey.

'Could it be,' asked the camel, 'that this Lord Jesus is some kind of king?'

'Oh certainly,' answered the donkey, 'he is the Christ child. On the night that He was born, the angels sang about him. He is King of the whole world, even though he is born in such a humble place, and he is called the Good Shepherd, which means he will look after us all, animals and people, as if we were all his sheep.' Well, the camel said nothing to that. He had never thought of himself as a sheep before and he had to consider the idea for a little while. It was all very strange. His master was a very wise man as well as a king. He must have known from his learning and from the signs in the sky that this was a special baby, as the donkey had said. 'How can I see this child for myself?' the camel asked. 'Around the side there is a little hole in the wall,' said the donkey, 'you can peep in there.'

So the tall stately camel squeezed around the side of the ramshackle building. He saw the hole in the wall that the donkey had mentioned. It was right down next to the ground. Slowly, the proud camel, who before would kneel only for his master, knelt down on the rough ground, and bowed his head right down so that he could peep in through the hole.

There was a soft light, like starlight in the shabby room, and there was Joseph: what a kind man he looked, he would never mistreat an animal! There was Mother Mary in her blue cloak, how beautiful she was. And there, in her arms, was the child whom they had travelled so far to find. How sweet and lovely he was, but oh how wonderful too! The proud camel could see at once that when this baby was a man, he would be the Good Shepherd who loved and cared for animals and people alike. The camel could also see his own master, kneeling before Mother Mary and the child, and bending his head low as he offered his precious gift. The proud camel knelt there looking for a long time, and then he quietly squeezed back around the building to the door.

When the wise king came out, he was surprised to see his proudest camel kneeling there with his head bent low to the ground. Mother Mary, carrying the Christ child in her arms, had come to the door too, to say goodbye to the royal visitors. And when the baby Jesus saw the camel bowing down, he laughed a lovely baby chuckle and waved his tiny hand. Mother Mary smiled to the camel too. Then the door was closed and it was time to begin the long journey home.

Well, for all the rest of his long life, that proud camel remembered how he had seen the Christ child and heard his lovely laugh as he knelt before him.

The Caterpillar

There was once a little caterpillar. Not a very special caterpillar, just a very ordinary one, and like every other ordinary caterpillar he just loved to eat. He ate leaves of every kind, sometimes flowers or vegetables – he really wasn't very fussy.

One day he happened to eat a very tasty leaf. Not only was it tasty, but it also made him feel healthier and bigger and stronger than he had ever felt before. He did not know that the leaf belonged to a myrrh bush that was particularly known for healing almost anything.

Anyway, the little caterpillar just loved the taste, so he ate and ate and ate. All of a sudden he heard a deep voice say: 'I will give a gift of myrrh!' and he felt the branch under him crack, and before he knew what was happening he was lifted into the air and put into a box, together with the branch of myrrh. The top of the box snapped shut, and there he was...in the dark. He could see nothing, absolutely nothing, but he was together with the branch of myrrh and this made him happy, for he could go on eating. This he did, but the strange thing was, that no matter how much he ate, the leaves grew again.

The box that he was in began to rock slowly from side to side and this made him sleepy, so he made himself a little silk cocoon to keep himself nice and cosy, and fell fast asleep.

How long he slept he did not know for he was having such pleasant dreams. Every now and then he woke a little and heard soft voices but the rocking put him to sleep again. At last the rocking stopped and a voice said: 'Our star has led us to this stable. We are here.' Then he felt as if he were falling, so he scrambled out of his cocoon and clung desperately to the myrrh branch. All of a sudden the lid of the box opened and the sun shone nice and warm upon him...but was it the sun? Where was the light coming from? He had to find out so he moved towards it and found that he was flying.

'A butterfly!' voices called out, 'and look at its golden wings!' Yes, the light was coming from the baby in the cradle. The butterfly flew round and round the little baby, in and out of the shining light and as he flew, so his wings became more and more golden. The baby laughed and tried to catch him and all the people there laughed too.

'What a beautiful gift!' said the lovely mother. 'Quite unexpected!' answered the wise king.

Verse for the Journey

Ever again upon the earth, and down from heaven high
We seek a place where we may rest, my holy child and I.
In every heart is hid a nest, wherein my child may lie,
So open your hearts to your baby guest, let in the heavens high.

The Flight into Egypt

In the days when the holy family rested in the little stable in Bethlehem, there lived a very wicked king who ruled the country. His name was King Herod.

King Herod heard that a little child had been born in a stable who would one day be greater than he, and that even kings had bowed down to this child and given him gifts of gold, frankincense and myrrh. King Herod was angry – very, very angry.

'I will find this baby and do away with him!' he shouted. 'No one can be a greater king than I! No one can be more powerful than I!' He called his soldiers together and he promised them much money if they could find the baby.

The angels, of course, knew what was happening and that it would be dangerous if Mary, Joseph and the baby remained in the stable. At night, when Joseph was fast asleep, an angel stood beside him and called to him: 'Joseph, awake! Joseph, awake! Take your family and go into Egypt. Go quickly, Joseph, for the soldiers are coming and want to harm your baby.'

Joseph woke up; then he woke Mary and told her what the angel had said and that they must leave at once.

It was the middle of the night and very cold, but the stars shone brightly in the heavens. Mary wrapped her baby in her blue cloak and Joseph helped her onto the donkey. They said goodbye to the stable and to all the dear creatures in it and thanked them all for the love and shelter they had given. Then, as quietly as they could, they made their way past the sleeping town onto the open road that led away from Bethlehem.

In the morning, when the soldiers came to the stable, all they found was an ox eating straw out of a manger. All the little creatures that were living there had made quite sure that there was nothing, not even one footprint, to show that anyone had been there.

Star Flowers

After leaving the stable, Mary and Joseph wandered through the winter countryside on their journey to Egypt. The fields and meadows were creaking with frost, rivers were frozen to ice, and icicles were hanging from bushes and trees. It was dark and the songbirds were still.

The woman walked slowly, for she carried a child in her arms. She pressed the baby against her red dress to keep it warm and held her blue cloak wrapped tightly about them to ward off the cold. The man walked in front with a lantern. They were looking for shelter, but far and wide there was nothing save the bare, hard earth, covered with stones and frost. The wind was fierce, tearing at cloak and hood and the cold was bitter, cracking the very stones.

Suddenly the man stopped. He pointed at something big and dark in front of them. 'Ah,' said the woman, 'God grant there is a house with a roof and a fire to warm ourselves.' And they made haste.

The path they had followed came to an end in front of a thick forest. They could not turn back as the howling wind had blown stones and trees across the path behind them. Weary and footsore, they made their way through the wall of trees and bushes into the dark forest. The wind rampaged about, making branches sigh and tree trunks bend.

It was past midnight when they came to a little clearing deep in the forest, where they sat down on an old log. There were no grass or flowers growing around their feet, nothing but stones and boulders and around them was the bare, black winter forest.

In her weariness, Mary did not notice how the angels of the clouds spread their heavy wings before the starry eyes of heaven, and how one snowflake after another flew down to earth, until her blue cloak was covered with white.

Suddenly, Mary heard a faint whisper near her ear. A snowflake had fallen into her hair and whispered softly: 'We come from your child's starry home, please look at us carefully. Could you find lovelier and more delicate stars? We would like to bring greetings to your child from his heavenly home.'

'Ah, you little messenger of the stars,' Mary said happily. She knelt down and took up into her hand a small piece of the frozen earth, which she raised to the sky. Then many, many snowflake stars settled on it.

Carefully, she opened her cloak a little to let the child look at the snow-covered earth in her hand. But as the child looked with the wonderful radiance of his eyes, a strange thing happened. The snow began to shape itself. In the mother's warm hand the icy earth had thawed, and tender roots stretched into it. Then, where the golden rays from the child's eyes shone into the shadow of the mother's hand, green stalks and leaves began to grow, and on the top blossomed a snow-white flower...a snow white Christmas rose had appeared!

Joseph and Mary were overjoyed as more and more white roses grew out of the snow around their feet, and, in the light shining all around them, they saw at last a little house; and there they rested.

The Holly Tree

One day, when Father Joseph and Mother Mary, with the Jesus child in her arms, were on the way to Egypt to escape from wicked King Herod, they looked back and saw Herod's soldiers following them along the road. The soldiers were coming nearer and nearer and there wasn't a house in sight, nor a tent, nor even a cave to hide in.

'Stop! Stop!' shouted the soldiers. Desperately they looked around, and Mary saw an old holly tree standing before her. 'Please give my baby a hiding place from these wicked

men,' she pleaded, and the holly tree opened wide and in went Mary with the baby and Joseph and the donkey too, and the tree closed itself and wrapped its leaves lovingly round the holy family. They stood there thankfully while the little baby slept, and they listened to what was going on outside.

The puzzled soldiers searched round and round, and got more and more angry. They could not even see Mary and Joseph's footprints, for the laughing wind had blown sand over them and into the eyes of the soldiers. The holly tree shook with laughter too, and when the soldiers got too close, it pricked them with its sharp leaves and swayed in the wind, till at last the soldiers got tired of looking and went back the way they had come.

When it was safe for the holy family to continue their journey, the holly tree opened itself wide, and as they departed Mary bowed to the kindly tree and said: 'Always you will remain evergreen and offer foliage, even in the depths of winter.'

And as you know, even today we can have green holly branches in our houses at Christmas time, for ever since it has kept its green mantle, even in the depths of winter.

The Hazel Bush

One day, when Mary and Joseph were fleeing from soldiers whom the wicked King Herod had sent to find the Jesus child, a strong wind was chasing dark clouds in the sky. Rain and lightning were coming nearer, and Mary held the baby safe in the warm folds of her cloak while Joseph led the donkey. They were looking for a house that would protect them but there was no tree to be seen, nor a place to shelter in. No building stood anywhere near, and there was not even an overhanging cliff to protect them. In the distance Joseph saw the branches of a tall hazel bush that stood near a hill. The branches were bending in the wind and swaying gently from side to side. Joseph guided the donkey towards it, hoping that it would shelter them all.

Mary wrapped her cloak more tightly round the child and crept under the hazel bush, which opened its branches like arms to protect them. It also gave shelter to Joseph and the donkey, which stood quietly by their side. Soon the rain was pouring down in sheets, lightning flashed in the sky and struck the earth all around them, but the bush protected them well. Its branches bent over the family, forming a roof of leaves. Not a drop of rain passed through and no lightning struck them.

When the storm had passed, they came out from under the branches. Mary smiled at the tree and thanked it. The holy family then continued on their journey.

Since that time, the hazel bush is said to be a safe place for a traveller caught in a storm, and lightning will never strike a person who seeks protection under its branches.

Leaven

Herod's soldiers were once again looking for Mary and the little child, and as she was fleeing from them she came to a house where the door stood open. There was a woman inside standing at a kneading trough, making dough for the bread.

'Oh, dear woman!' Mary called out fearfully, 'help me to hide my child. Look, there in the street where the dust is whirling, the soldiers are coming and they want to take my child from me!'

The woman asked: 'Shall I put him under the blanket?' 'Oh no, the soldiers will pierce through it with a sword!' cried Mary. 'Shall I put him into a cupboard?' 'Oh no,' cried Mary fearfully, 'they will open it!'

'Give him to me, I will put him into the baking trough and spread dough over him,' said the woman. Mary nodded, and quickly put the child into the baking trough where the woman covered him with the bread dough.

Hardly had his little hands and feet disappeared, when the door flew open with a crash. Bearded soldiers stepped into the little house and looked gloomily around. They rolled their eyes and shouted: 'Is the child here? Give him to us!'

The baking woman put herself bravely in front of those rough men and said: 'I am too old to have children! Mine have long grown up and gone out into the world. Look around for yourselves, you will not find children here!'

How the soldiers looked! Under the table, under the benches, they pierced their swords through the bed and cut open the pillows so that feathers flew into the air. They opened the cupboards, tipped over the water jugs and looked everywhere, but nowhere could they find a child. Meanwhile, Mary was kneading dough as if she was the maid of the house and she did not once look up.

When the soldiers did not find anything, they broke a big water jug that was standing near the trough and, stamping loudly, they went out of the door shouting rude words.

The baking woman ran over to the trough. 'Oh wonder!' she called out. 'Look how much the dough has risen; it is nearly flowing over the edge!' She took the little boy out and put him into Mary's arms. She then started to shape loaf after loaf from the dough.

Mary held her son and cuddled him: 'Always keep a little left-over bit from this dough for the next time,' she said, 'then the new dough will also rise.' Then she thanked the woman and left the house.

Mary had already gone a long way on her journey, and the woman was still forming loaves. There was enough to feed all the people in the whole village, but the last little bit of dough the woman put aside for the next baking day.

A week later, when the baking woman was kneading bread at the trough again, she did not forget to put the little left-over bit of dough from before into the new dough, even though it had, in the meantime, turned sour. Again the dough rose to the edge of the baking trough.

Many people came and asked for some of this wonderful dough, so that their bread would also grow and grow from day to day. And the same happened for them.

Even today, bakers knead a little of the old dough into the new; and to this day the bread rises and multiplies because of it, and they call it sourdough bread.

The Holly Bush

When Mary, Joseph, the baby and the donkey left Bethlehem, their way led through a forest. Suddenly they heard behind them the sound of many loud, harsh voices. Mary quickly rushed to a bush and hid the baby in between the soft green leaves. She ran a little distance away and started to collect some wood in her cloak as if she were a poor woman from the village, while Joseph loaded dry twigs onto the donkey.

Indeed, King Herod's soldiers were coming this way, searching everywhere for the baby. Mary could see their wild faces, their armour glinting in the light and their swords clanking at their sides as they walked. She became terribly frightened and started trembling all over. Her heart was thumping loudly and she glanced at the bush. Most of the soldiers had already gone ahead into the forest, but one was watching her and saw where she looked. He laughed and went over to the green bush where the child lay hidden. He stretched his naked arms into the leaves to pull them apart, but at that moment he screamed loudly, then shouting rude words he ran after his companions. Drops of blood were running down his arms.

When he had disappeared into the forest, Mary ran to the bush. Now she discovered the reason why the soldier had screamed, for all the leaves of the bush had become hard and sharp and there were little points just like thorns on the edges of the leaves. These thorny leaves had pricked the soldier terribly, and had scratched and torn at his arms. With a stick, Joseph carefully pushed the branches aside and Mary freed her child without any harm from the little bush that had protected him so well.

Since then, the holly tree has green leaves all the year round, and the red berries which it bears in the winter remind us of the drops of blood which Herod's soldier shed when he scratched his arms on the sharp edged leaves. We call this holy bush, the holly bush.

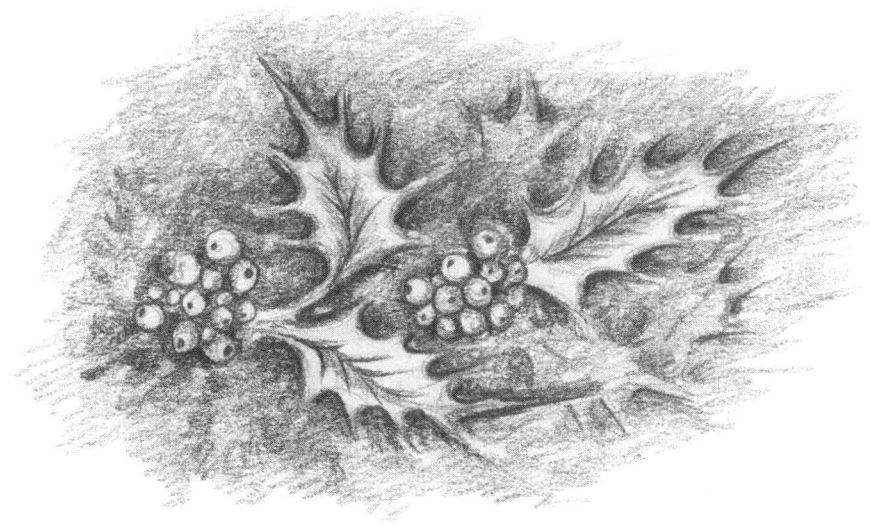

The Story of the Wagtail

While the holy family were on their journey to Egypt, wicked King Herod sent his soldiers after them. They had reached the desert, and Joseph's footsteps and the donkey's hooves had left clear marks in the sand. It wasn't long before the footprints were spotted by the soldiers. A soldier called out: 'Look here in the sand, this is the footprint of a man, and here is a donkey whose hooves have made very deep imprints! Surely the mother is sitting on the donkey with the boy – they cannot be far!'

The soldiers whipped their horses to go faster and followed the footprints in the sand. A little wagtail (a very small bird) had been flying past and heard what the soldiers said. Quickly it flew, much faster than the horses could travel, until it came to where Joseph was leading the donkey through the desert. The wagtail saw how they moved slowly and steadily through the sand, Mary holding the precious child on her lap, sheltering him from the hot sun that shone on them during the day. The little bird flew down and, with quick movements of its tail, it wiped out the marks of the footprints in the sand. For a long time it worked, following the trail which led towards the approaching soldiers. Then with a swoop, it flew into the air above the soldiers, waiting to see what they would do.

All of a sudden, the soldiers came to a stop in the middle of a sand-dune. They looked around, shouting to each other, looking in every direction to see where the footprints had gone...they had disappeared! The angry soldiers shouted at the wind which they thought had blown away the footprints, and looked everywhere – except up, where the little wagtail chirped gaily and wagged its tail in glee.

Well, do you know, even today that little bird's tail goes up and down without tiring, as if smoothing the sand over the holy family's footprints. That is why we call it the wagtail.

The Turtle Bridge

At the time when Mary and Joseph were on their way to Egypt, Joseph needed to go and buy some food. He did not want to go into the village with Mary and the child, for he knew that the wicked King Herod's soldiers were searching for the holy family. Joseph said to Mary: 'This seems to be a place where no one would come, for it is swampy and muddy. You could wait here under the shade of a tree, and I will take the donkey and go and get some food from the village.' Mary agreed, for she was grateful for the rest, and so sat waiting patiently for his return.

While Joseph was away, however, the soldiers had discovered Mary's footprints and were nearing the swamp. She could hear them calling to each other and the clink of their swords as they cut through the reeds. Mary looked this way and that, but there was no path to follow through the swamp and she could not go back the way she had come. The only way was through the swamp, but each time she put her feet down the mud sucked at them and she could hardly move.

Mary nearly lost heart, when from all around turtles came crawling slowly out of the swamp. Soon they had formed a row, making a bridge across the swamp. On their backs Mary walked: across the swamp she went, and soon she reached the other side and stepped once more onto firm ground. She thanked the turtles, who disappeared once more under the muddy water.

Mary quickly hid herself behind a tree and watched to see what would happen. It wasn't long before the soldiers arrived at the swamp and saw Mary's footsteps leading to the muddy water's edge. They ran into the water, but sank into the mud that sucked at their legs, and soon they were up to their knees in it and could hardly move. It was only with great difficulty that they turned and went back to the firm ground again, helping each other with ropes and sticks to climb out of the sticky mud. Some lost their boots and came out bare-footed, and they were all covered with brown, sticky mud. They were cross, grumbling and mumbling to each other: 'They couldn't have gone this way, no one can, it's impossible!' they said, and sat in the grass cleaning themselves. Then they turned around and went back the way they had come.

Beside a nearby palm tree Joseph and Mary found each other again, and Mary blessed the turtles who had helped them in their distress. Then they went on their way.

The Palm Tree

Mary, Joseph, the baby and the little donkey had been on the road for many days during their flight through Egypt. They were escaping from the soldiers whom King Herod had sent to capture them. One day they came to a dry, bare part of the land. Neither trees nor bushes grew there anymore and the rays of the sun had dried up the grass. Soon there was only desert spread before them – sand, sand, and more sand stretched endlessly for miles and miles before them. No cool wind blew any more, and the rays of the sun shone hotter and hotter onto the dry earth.

Mary could hardly stay upright on the donkey, and Joseph was sweating heavily. The donkey drooped its ears and walked along with lowered head. In the shade of Mary's cloak lay the slumbering child, and from time to time the mother gently fanned some air over his hot little face. The travellers were suffering from thirst, for there was not one drop of water left in the water bag which Joseph carried. He was very worried about this, especially as the desert seemed endless.

Suddenly the donkey lifted its head and shook its ears. Looking up, Mary saw a palm tree in the distance near a sandy hill. The donkey walked faster to get into the shade of the tree, and Joseph was left quite a distance behind. When they arrived, Mary climbed down from the donkey and laid the baby on her cloak in the shade of the palm tree. Up, on top of the tree, hung the most beautiful dates. 'Ah,' she said to Joseph, when he arrived panting from the heat, 'if only we had some of that fruit!' 'Well, Mary,' answered Joseph, 'I wish I could work miracles, but you see the tree is rather high so I can't possibly get any down.'

'Please give me a little drink of water then, I am terribly thirsty,' said Mary. Rather worried, Joseph answered: 'We drank the last drop when we had our rest, before we arrived in the desert.'

While they were talking to each other, the little hands of the child waved up to the palm tree and the boy called in a delicate singing voice: 'Come tree, bend down to me!' Then the tall palm tree slowly bent down towards the earth until the dates reached right into Mary's hand. She picked the sweet fruit with great joy, and Joseph filled a bag to the very top for the journey.

When Mary, Joseph and the child ate the fruit, they became very thirsty. At the foot of this palm tree a wind had blown away the sand, so that a root, as thick as an arm,

stuck out of the earth. For a second time the little hand appeared and beckoned to the root. 'Give water,' the little voice sang. Then water started trickling down from the root like a small spring. The water was cool, fresh and pure, and they all drank their fill. Joseph filled up the water bag again, and still the water did not stop flowing.

Mary dug out the sand between the roots of the palm and made a little pool with her hands, and she bathed the little child in it. His cheeks had been covered with grey dust from the desert, but as he splashed in the cool water they became fresh and pink as roses again.

Now the donkey came nearer too and drank, shaking his ears and swishing his tail happily.

When they left that sheltered oasis in the desert, the spring continued to flow from the roots of the palm tree.

And from that day onwards, travellers who passed that place were able to refresh themselves at Mary's Palm, for that was the name it was given for evermore.

The Spider and the Fly

The wicked King Herod had promised lots of money to those who would find the holy child, for he would not believe that this child who was born in a stable could grow up to be the king of the people who lived in his kingdom. He was the king, and no one else!

One day when the holy family were on their way to Egypt, trying to escape from King Herod's soldiers, they rested by the roadside and then fell asleep. So they did not hear the tramp, tramp, tramp of the soldiers' feet as they came gradually nearer. They did not realise it, but a fly was looking after the family and from a treetop he had seen the soldiers coming.

He buzzed around Joseph's head, but the old man slept on. Then the little fly thought there was no time to be polite anymore, so he alighted right on the tip

of his nose! Of course Joseph awoke with a start and then he, too, could hear the tramp of the soldiers. Very worried, he looked around and saw a cave that seemed to be well hidden. Hastily he led his family into the cave and seated Mary deep inside the cave, as far as possible from the light of the entrance. However, the little fly was not satisfied. She went to her old enemy the spider and said: 'Quick, quick, what can we do to save them?'

'I know,' said the clever spider, 'I will spin a web right across the entrance to the cave and you can blow dust on it to make it look old.' The spider worked so quickly and so skilfully that by the time the soldiers rode by, it heard their leader say: 'It's no use looking in that cave, there's a dusty old spider's web across the entrance, obviously no one has been there for at least a week, so hurry on, my men, hurry on!'

When Mary and Joseph had rested, they said tender words of gratitude to the tiny creatures who had helped them, and the little child reached out his hand and touched the spider on its back.

To this day the little spider proudly bears a cross upon its back, reminding us of its brave deed.

The Poplar and the Holly

Long ago, when Joseph and Mother Mary and the Jesus child were fleeing to Egypt, they heard the sound of galloping horses, and the shouts of Herod's soldiers coming close behind them: 'There they are! There they are! We will bring them to Herod our King!'

Mother Mary, hearing the galloping horses, asked a tall poplar tree for help, hoping that its broad sweeping branches would protect the holy family. However, the tree feared harm to itself; and, thinking that the cruel soldiers would cut it down, it lifted its shivering and shaking branches to the sky, to show the soldiers that no one was hiding beneath them.

Now near this fearful tree stood a soft, green bush with white berries.

'Come quickly to me. I will shelter you as best I can,' the bush called out to the holy family, and they quickly hid between the leaves. And the soft, green bush protected the holy family with her branches, which she closed around them.

While Herod's soldiers came closer and closer, the brave little bush gathered its strength and grew bigger and bigger. Its soft, green leaves grew hard, and from them sharp, pointed prickles sprouted like spears.

The soldiers were searching the whole area, for they knew the holy family had hidden somewhere nearby, and one of them glimpsed a bit of the red of Mother Mary's dress in the bush. He called to the others and they stretched their hands into the bush to seize the baby, but the sharp prickles pierced their skin and they could not break through the tangle of branches, which grew so thickly together.

'Those are only berries. No one could hide in such a prickly bush! They have escaped!' shouted one of the soldiers. 'Get on your horses and ride. We will soon catch up with them.' And away they rode.

And to this day, the holy bush or holly, as we now call it, can grow into a tall tree with hard leaves brandishing sharp prickles, and bearing beautiful shiny berries that are deep red like Mother Mary's dress. The berries remind us of how the brave holly once sheltered the holy family.

And what of the tall poplar tree? Well, it still shivers and shakes and stands rooted like a tower, lifting its head to the clouds, longing for the day when it can again lower its branches and caress the earth.

The Poor Little Girl

Near a village, there was a big stone lying in a field. Every morning, a little jug with milk and a piece of bread was placed upon it.

Every day, early in the morning, a little girl came out of the forest and walked towards the stone, then taking the little jug and bread she disappeared again behind the trees.

Why did she go back so sadly into the forest? A little while ago she had still been living with her father and mother in the village, but an ugly illness had covered her skin with sores, and the people in the village said: 'That child must go away into the forest. She can't stay with us any longer, otherwise we will also get this nasty illness.'

And so it happened that the poor girl had to leave her home. Now she was living between bushes in a hollow tree-trunk. Every morning her father put the bread and the little jug with milk on the stone in the field for her. The poor little girl found some berries in the forest to eat with her bread, and she had to make do with just this.

Towards this village Mary and Joseph came with the Jesus child. The boy was thirsty but nowhere could Mary find anything for him to drink, and she said: 'Don't worry, my little child, we will soon be at the next village.' Before they reached the village, they nearly bumped into the poor girl just as she was carefully carrying the little jug into the forest.

She had heard Mary's wish and she brought her little jug and gave it to her, saying softly: 'Here, take from this milk, for I heard you say your little boy was thirsty.' Mary let the little boy drink. Gratefully she stroked the girl's hair, and giving her some dates, they rode further on their way.

When the little girl came to the hollow tree she also wanted to drink. She looked into the jug and saw, with astonishment, that the jug was full again. She ate some of the dates and drank from the milk, which tasted much sweeter than it ever had before. Hardly had she drunk when the sores disappeared from her face and hands.

She ran to a little pool of water, looked into it, and saw with wonder her shining healthy face, without sores, looking back at her.

Taking her jug she ran like a deer to the village. 'Mother! Father!' she called out, 'I am healed! I am healed!'

Her mother and father came running out of the house and embraced their child with great joy.

Soon all the people in the neighbourhood gathered to touch her clean, delicate smooth skin with their fingers. Over and over again she told the story about the wonderful miracle, and showed the little jug, which always stayed full of fresh sweet milk.

And from that day on, if any ill person drank from that jug, they were also healed.

The Daisy or Mary Flower

A few days before Jesus' third birthday, his mother Mary wanted to make him a crown of flowers to wear on the special day. Wherever she looked, in woods, meadows and on the hillsides, there were no flowers to be found, for the frost and cold of midwinter had taken them all. So she decided to make the flowers from cloth.

Mary cut out many petals from white satin, and sewed little flowers with golden silk in the centre. Jesus watched her all the time as she made this flowery crown. While sewing the white petals onto the golden centre, Mary pricked her finger and some of the white petals became tipped with red. Jesus loved this crown the best of all his presents and he wore it all day on his birthday, and treasured it carefully through the whole winter.

When spring came, he planted the crown of cloth flowers in the earth and watered them from a golden cup, which had been brought to him by one of the Three Wise Kings at his birth. He then blew his breath over them and watched over them with love.

The little white flowers with golden centres took root and grew.

Gradually they spread all over the earth and have become one of the most loved flowers. They are called the 'Days-eyes' or 'Daisies', for as the sun sinks to rest in the evening, so the daisy's white petals close over the golden centre; then open again in the morning at sunrise. They are also known as 'Mary Flowers'.

Children still make crowns or chains from them, in memory of the one that Mary made for Jesus on his third birthday.

The White Bird

Once upon a time, in a far distant land, there lived a poor woodcutter and his wife. They had a little hut in a clearing in a dark forest. Sometimes they were hungry; for although they had a little garden around their house, they could only grow a few herbs and shade-loving plants. The trees that surrounded the clearing were so tall that the sun could seldom shine into their little plot, so flowers and vegetables did not grow at all easily.

The only living creature they had was a thin little cow. It gave just enough milk to drink with the small amount of bread they were able to make from the wheat growing in a corner of the clearing. In winter, when thick snow covered the land and ice formed along the branches of the trees, the woodcutter hardly found enough wood for a fire, so often they were cold as well as hungry.

Now the woodcutter's wife, I am sorry to say, was rather a crosspatch. She often grumbled because their life was so poor and hard and because the sun hardly shone for them. 'If only we were rich, oh if only we had beautiful clothes,' she would say, 'if only we had a child to keep us company.' She complained so bitterly that the woodcutter was sometimes quite downcast and unhappy.

One Christmas Eve, when the woodcutter was out in the forest, he took his big axe and began to swing it in order to cut down a certain tree. Now this tree was hollow, and as he swung the axe for the first blow, he heard a faint sound coming from within. He put down the axe and looked into the hole, and there he saw a most beautiful white bird. It was faint and weak from having to struggle to free its foot from a tangle of creepers which wound all around it. The woodcutter gently freed the bird and lifted it out. He was astonished at its beauty, for besides the perfect white of its feathers, it had a lovely proud head with jewel-like eyes, and it seemed to him that a star glowed faintly on its brow. Carefully he carried the white bird home to his wife, though he expected to be met with grumbling and scolding. 'What have you there?' asked his wife rather crossly. He showed her the bird and immediately her heart felt a little less frozen and icy when she saw the lovely creature.

So she did not scold her husband, but fetched a branch from the clearing, put it in a corner of the hut near the hearth and let the bird perch on it, feeding it breadcrumbs and water.

That night the woodcutter's wife had a dream. She dreamt that an angel, clad in white, with a star on its forehead, appeared before her and said: 'If there can be peace and harmony, love and happiness in this dwelling for a year and a day, then will your heart's desire be granted.' Then the angel vanished.

The next day, as the woman was sweeping her floor, she knocked the broom sharply against the wall, so that the handle broke. She was just about to scold and speak crossly, when she remembered her dream and, making a great effort, she kept silent and would not allow the sharp words to come from her mouth. Then she felt her frozen heart thawing still more, and she saw, too, that the star on the white bird's head was beginning to glow softly.

Time passed, and there came a cold and windy day in spring. There was still snow on the ground and the forest creatures were hard put to find enough food. At mid-day, just as the woodcutter and his wife were sitting down to their humble dinner, which consisted of a bowl of milk and a slice of bread each, they heard a faint scratching at the door and the sound of a weak 'miaow'. Opening the door, the woodcutter saw a poor shivering little wild forest cat looking at him wistfully. It was so weak from hunger it was scarcely able to miaow. He picked it up, turned to his wife and said: 'Let's give this little creature something to eat.'

In the past his wife would have answered sharply and said that there was scarcely enough for themselves, how could they spare anything? But now her heart was softer, and she remembered the dream of the angel. So she said: 'Yes, gladly – come little cat, take my bread and milk and sit here by the fire.' The little creature came in, lapped the milk and bread and curled up by the fire. And immediately, with the golden star glowing more brightly still, the white bird lifted its head and trilled: 'Joy, joy, joy, joy, joy, joy, joy.'

Time passed and there came a day in summer when the herbs and flowers in the garden were in bloom. As evening was falling, the woodcutter and his wife heard a knock at their door. There stood an old, old beggar woman, clad in rags. She was tired and hungry. The woodcutter asked her in and his wife gave the old woman her own share of the supper and also gave her a cloak to wear to cover her rags. As soon as she had done this, the white bird trilled once again: 'Red roses for love, red roses for love! Joy, joy, joy, joy, joy, joy, joy!' And when the woodcutter and his wife looked at it they saw that the star was shining more brightly than before, and on the branch where it perched was a beautiful red rose in bloom.

Time passed, and it was Christmas Eve again. The year and a day were nearly over. Snow lay on the ground once more. As the woodcutter and his wife were about to go to sleep that night, they heard a knock at their door. The woodcutter went to open it and there stood a little child.

They were astonished to see someone so young and fair alone in the forest on a winter's night and they brought him in and took him near to the fire to keep him warm. At that moment the last bit of ice in the woman's heart melted, and it was filled with love and only love. She gave the child her most precious possessions – these were the little cat, which was now tame, and a beautiful Christmas rose, which she had grown in a pot and tended with great care for many weeks.

Then all around there was the sound of most wonderful music. It seemed as if all the violins and lyres and flutes in the world were singing together, and above it all came the sound of the white bird's song: 'Peace at Christmas, peace at Christmas! Red roses for love, red roses for love! Joy, joy, joy, joy, joy, joy, joy!' The star on its forehead shone so brightly that the woodcutter and his wife were quite dazzled by the light and had to shut their eyes for a moment. When they opened them and looked at the corner where the white bird lived on its branch, they saw that the whole branch was covered with beautiful red roses, which scented the air. The white bird had vanished, but in its place stood the little child, clad all in white and with a golden star on its brow.

Then the woodcutter and his wife knew that this was their longed-for son and that they had been granted their heart's desire.

Do you know what they called their little son? They called him 'Star Child'!

The Silver Flute

There was once a young boy called Luke who lived with his mother and father in a little house behind his father's shop. He loved to spend hours in the shop, for his father had so many lovely things to sell. There were toys and pictures, chairs and vases, violins and lamps, and even a little drum.

Luke had one wish that he wished more than anything else in the whole world, and that was to play music to the Christ child. He took a little violin in his father's shop and tried to play it, but hard as he tried all that he could get out of it were terrible squeaks – and, of course, that would never do. He even tried to play the little drum, but that only made a noise, for one cannot really play tunes on a drum! 'Oh dear,' said Luke, 'that would never do, I don't think my wish will ever come true.'

One day when he was in his father's shop, a poor old man knocked on the door. He was carrying a sack that was full and heavy. His father opened the door and the old man came in and put the heavy sack down on the floor with a thump. 'I am very hungry,' said the old man, 'please will you buy whatever is in my sack so that I can then buy myself some food?'

Luke's father was very kind, and felt sorry for the poor old man. 'Of course I will,' he said, 'I will buy everything you have.' And he gave the old man some money. The old man was very pleased and thanked him very much. Then, leaving the sack in the middle of the floor, out he went.

Luke's father emptied the sack. There was not very much in it, just some old clothes, pots and an old flute. 'Here you are, Luke,' said his father, and he gave Luke the little flute. The old clothes and pots he put out on the shelves to sell.

Luke was very pleased. Perhaps now if he tried very hard he would be able to play the little flute well enough to play to the child.

For hours every day he played his little flute, but no matter how hard he tried, or for how long, all he could play were harsh noises, for the flute was far too old. 'Perhaps someone else will have better luck than I,' he said, and he put the little flute in the window to sell.

'You are a kind boy, Luke,' said a little voice; and there, sitting on the flute was a tiny fairy. 'I am the fairy of the flute,' she said, 'and I know your dearest wish; and because you are so kind I will help you. If you take the flute and dip it into the water of the little river which runs next to the old oak tree in the forest, it will turn into pure silver. But mind, it must be done as the first ray of moonlight touches the water.'

'Oh thank you, fairy, thank you,' said Luke. 'But if that is to happen I shall have to hurry, for soon the sun will be setting and the river is quite far away.' Luke took the little flute and, with the fairy sitting on it, he hurried out of the shop.

On he walked, out of the town and along the road to the forest. As he walked along, he heard a little voice crying: 'Miaow, help me! Miaow, help me!' He looked up and

saw that high in a branch of a tree sat a little kitten. She had climbed up the tree after a little bird, and was now too frightened to come down again. 'Don't worry little kitten, I will help you,' called Luke. 'Luke,' said the flute fairy, 'you are a good boy, but if you stop to help the kitten you will not be in time to dip the flute into the river as the first moonbeam touches the water.'

'I must stop to help the kitten first,' said Luke, 'and then if I walk very fast I will still be in time.' So up the tree he climbed, took hold of the kitten under one arm and climbed down again. The kitten scampered off happily. 'Now I must hurry,' he said, and walked very fast.

Soon he came to a fence and as he was climbing over it he heard a funny little noise. He looked down and there he saw a little bunny that had caught its hind foot in the fence and could not get it free. 'I will help you, little bunny,' he said. 'Luke,' said the flute fairy, 'you are a good boy, but if you stop to help the bunny you will not be in time to dip the flute into the river as the first moonbeam touches the water.' 'Then afterwards I will run!' said Luke. 'But first I must help the bunny.'

He knelt down and loosened the bunny's leg, but oh, it was scratched and bleeding. He took his handkerchief and bound it around the bunny's sore foot. The bunny wiggled its ears to say 'Thank you' – and off he hopped.

Now Luke had to run for he was very late and the sun had already set. Soon he saw the oak tree; how happy he was for he was just in time. He came to the river but as he knelt down to dip the flute into the water he heard: 'Twee, tweeee.' He looked up into the oak tree and saw that a little bird had caught its wing in a branch and was fluttering hard to free itself. 'Wait, little bird,' Luke called, 'you will hurt your wing if you flutter so. I will help you.'

'Luke,' called the flute fairy, 'you are a good boy but if you help the little bird you will not be in time to dip the flute into the river as the first moonbeam touches the water, for I see the moon rising.' 'Well,' said Luke, 'it is far better that I help the little bird.' He climbed up the tree and loosened the little bird's wing from the branch.' 'Thank you, Luke, thank you,' chirped the little bird, and off he flew.

As Luke climbed down the tree he saw the first moonbeam touch the water – he was too late! He held the little flute in his hands. 'Now I shall have to forget my wish about playing music for the child,' he said sadly, and two tears fell down his cheeks and on to the flute, and as they touched the flute a wonderful thing happened. It started to sparkle, and then to shine, and then – wonder of wonders – it turned to pure gold!

'Had you done as I said and dipped the flute into the river as the first moonbeam touched the water, your flute would have turned to silver,' said the flute fairy. 'But because you are such a good boy and have helped others instead, your flute has turned to gold. Play it now, dear Luke.'

Luke put the flute to his lips and blew, and out came music so beautiful and pure, more pure even than the singing of a nightingale. Luke was so happy that light shone from his eyes. Now at last his wish would be granted...and I am sure it was – aren't you?

The Christmas Tree Song

This song can be sung to the tune of 'O Tannenbaum'.
It can be sung before or after the Christmas tree stories, 'to make the tree happy'.

O woodland tree, O pinewood tree,

How fresh and green your branches.

Not only in the summer time,

But mid the winter's frost and rime.

O woodland tree, O pinewood tree,

How fresh and green your branches.

O woodland tree, O Christmas tree,

How gaily decked your branches.

The many candles lovely light

Is shed around for our delight.

O Christmas tree, bright Christmas tree,

We bless your happy branches.

The Too-little Fir Tree

Once upon a time there was a little fir tree, slim, pointed and shiny. It stood in a great forest in the midst of some big fir trees that were broad and tall and shady green. The little fir tree was very unhappy because he was not big like the others.

When the birds came flying into the woods and sat on the branches of the big trees and built their nests there, he used to call up to them: 'Come down, come down and nest in my branches!' but the birds said: 'Oh no, you are too little!'

When the splendid wind came blowing and singing through the forest, it bent and rocked and swung the tops of the big trees, and murmured to them. Then the little fir tree looked up and called: 'Oh, please, dear wind, come down and play with me!' But the wind always said: 'Oh no, you are too little, you are too little!'

In the winter when the white snow fell softly and covered the great trees all over with wonderful caps and coats of white, the little fir tree, down under the branches of the others, would call up: 'Oh please, dear snow, give me a cap too! I also want to play!' but the snow said: 'Oh no, you are too little, you are too little!'

Worst of all was when men came into the wood with carts and horses in order to cut the big trees down and carry them away. Whenever one had been cut down and carried away, the others talked about it and nodded their heads. The little fir tree listened, and heard them say that when you were carried away you might become the mast of a mighty sailing ship and go far away over the ocean and see many wonderful things. Or you might be part of a fine house in a great city, and see much of life. The little fir tree wanted so much to see life, but he was always too little to be carried away.

One cold winter's morning men came with a cart and horses, and after they had cut here and there they came to the circle of trees around the little fir tree, and looked around. 'There are none little enough,' they said. Oh, how the little fir tree pricked up his needles! 'Here is one,' said one man, 'it is just little enough.' And he touched the little fir tree.

The little fir tree was so happy. When he was being carried away on the cart he lay wondering whether he would become the mast of a ship or part of a fine city house. They came to the town and he was taken out of the cart and set upright in a tub. He

was placed on the edge of a path in a row of other fir trees. All were small, but none so little as he. And then the little fir tree began to see life.

People kept coming to look at the trees and to take them away, but always when they saw the little fir tree they shook their heads and said: 'It is too little, too little.'

Two little children came along, hand in hand, looking carefully at all the small trees. When they saw the little fir tree they cried out: 'We'll take this one for it is just little enough!'

They carried him away between them, and the happy little fir tree spent all his time wondering what it could be that he was just little enough for. He knew it could hardly be the mast of a ship or part of a house, since he was going away with children.

He kept on wondering, while they took him into a house and placed him on the table in a bare little room. Very soon they went away, and came back with a big basket, which they carried between them. The children took things out of the basket and began to play with the little fir tree, just as he had often begged the wind and the snow and the birds to do. He felt their soft little touches on his twigs and his branches and when he looked down at himself he saw that he was all hung with gold and silver chains! His twigs held little gold nuts and silver stars and tiny toys. He had pretty red and white candles on his branches and, most wonderful of all, the children had hung a beautiful white doll-angel on his highest branch! The little fir tree could hardly breathe for joy and wonder. What was he now? Why was this glory for him?

After a time every one went away and he was left alone. It grew darker, and the little fir tree began to hear strange sounds through the closed doors. He was beginning to feel lonely. All at once the doors opened and the two children came in. Two ladies were with them. They came up to the little fir tree and lit all the little candles. Then the two ladies took hold of the table with the little fir tree on it and pushed it very smoothly and quietly out of the doors, across the hall, and into another room.

The little fir tree entered a long room with many little beds in it, and there were children propped up on pillows in the beds. Other children sat in wheelchairs, and others hobbled about or sat on little chairs. He wondered why all the little children looked so pale and tired. He did not know that he was in a hospital. But before he could wonder any more his breath was quite taken away by the shout that those pale little children gave.

'Oh! Oh! Look!' they cried. 'How pretty! How beautiful! Oh, isn't it lovely!

He knew they must mean him, for all their shining eyes were looking at him. He stood as straight as a mast, and every needle quivered for joy. Then one little weak voice called out: 'It's the nicest Christmas tree I ever saw!'

And then, at last, the little fir tree knew what he was. He was a Christmas tree! And from his shiny head to his roots he was happy through and through, because he was just little enough to be the nicest kind of tree in the world – a Christmas tree!

The Fir Tree's Gift

On the night that Jesus was born three trees stood outside the stable. They were talking together in whispers. The tall palm tree said rather proudly: 'We must give him gifts. I know what I shall give him – a bunch of dates. He and Mother Mary will love my sweet juicy dates. What are you going to give him?' The gnarled old olive tree replied: 'My gift shall be some of my olives – Father Joseph will press them and give the oil that comes from them to Mother Mary, and she will use it in many ways for her son. I am sure my gift of olives will be useful.' Then both trees turned to the third, a very young fir tree, and said: 'Now what can you give as a present? You are so small, you have no fruit and even if you were big enough, you would only have hard cones and they are of no use to anyone. You haven't even any leaves, just sharp needles that would prick the baby if he touched you. Poor thing! We don't know what you can give!'

The little fir tree was sad and would have liked to sink into the ground and hide itself. It murmured softly: 'I love him as much as you two big trees.' However, they did not hear, for they were wondering when Joseph would come out of the stable to pick their dates and olives.

Meanwhile it grew very cold. Jack Frost came by with his freezing breath and everything he touched became coated in silver and white. He covered the three trees with frost and ice and they all looked beautiful, but the little fir tree sparkled in the starlight with its many needles, each outlined with frost. Mary looked out of the stable and was astonished at its beauty.

At dawn, Jesus awoke and looked out at the frosty world. The first thing he saw was the little fir tree sparkling and glittering with silvery frost. He clapped his tiny hands with joy and laughed with pleasure. Mary said: 'Little fir tree, you have given my son a real gift, see how delighted he is at your beauty. Thank you, little fir tree!'

Both the palm and the olive trees bent down and whispered: 'You have given him the best gift of all.'

And that is one of the reasons why we always have fir trees as our Christmas trees.

The Wishes of the Fir Tree

Once upon a time there was a little fir tree. He lived in a forest with many other different kinds of trees. Now the little fir tree was very, very sad because he did not like his pine needles. He thought they were too prickly.

'All the other trees have nice soft leaves,' he grumbled, 'why do I have to have needles instead of leaves?' And sticky tears dropped down all his pine needles.

'Why are you so sad?' said a tiny little voice, and there in front of him stood a little fairy.

'I am sad because my leaves are sharp and pointy,' wept the little tree. 'I will give you one wish,' said the fairy. 'You can wish for any kind of leaves you like.' The little tree said: 'I would like some nice soft leaves, please.' So the little fairy clapped her hands and all of a sudden the fir tree was covered in soft green leaves. Oh, how happy he was! 'Thank you, thank you, kind fairy,' he said. But while he stood there so happy in his new green leaves, along came a goat.

'Baa,' said the goat, 'look at those lovely green leaves, they are just what I need to eat because I am so hungry.' And he ate up all the little green leaves. The little fir tree stood there with nothing on and now he cried even harder.

Along came the fairy. 'What kind of leaves would you like now?' she said. The fir tree thought a little bit and then said: 'I wish for nice silver leaves.' The little fairy clapped her hands and the tree was covered with nice little silver leaves, which tinkled softly in the wind. Now how happy the little tree was! He tinkled his leaves so that all the trees could hear him.

Children loved to play in the forest, and it wasn't long before they also heard the tinkling of the leaves. They came running up to the little tree and in great delight they took all the leaves off and ran laughing, happily tinkling their little leaves all the way home.

Now the little tree really wept because he was once more poor and bare. Again the little fairy came along and said: 'One last wish, little tree. What kind of leaves do you want now?' The little tree thought hard and said, 'please will you give me leaves of gold?' The little fairy clapped her hands and soon the little tree was covered with golden leaves. How beautifully he shone and glittered in the sun. He thought he looked absolutely wonderful!

Soon a poor man came by. He had a bag over his shoulder and was looking for food, and when he saw the golden tree he thought: 'Ah, now I can pick those leaves and sell them to buy food for my children so that they won't ever be hungry again.' He picked all the leaves, then put them in his bag and walked home.

Once again the little tree stood with his branches all bare, and he was so sad that he could not even weep any more. The fairy appeared once more: 'What now, little tree?' she asked.

'How I wish I was a little fir tree again,' he said. 'I will be so happy to have my prickly green pine needles back once more.' The fairy clapped her hands and there he was, covered all over in pine needles again.

He was very happy to be a little fir tree once more, and stood in the forest, proudly flourishing his prickly branches. Soon he heard footsteps, and along came a man with a big spade. He came up to the little tree, walked around it, looked it up and down and said: 'Yes, this one will be very nice.' And he dug up the little fir tree! The little fir tree started to shiver, and wondered what was going to happen.

Well, the man put the tree on a donkey cart and took it away to his house where he planted it in a little tub. He took the fir tree inside a big room and closed the door secretly. Then he hung small, shiny red apples, gold and silver tinsel, little glass balls of many colours and tiny presents wrapped in patterned paper. Before he finished, he also placed candles carefully all over the prickly branches and put a beautiful star at its very tip, then he left the room.

All was very quiet for a long, long time. Then, when it was dark, the man came in and lit the candles. Soon there came the joyous shouts and laughter of many little children. They came into the room and stood around the little tree, looking at it in wonder. It was the most beautiful tree they had ever seen. They sang carols, played games, opened presents and told stories; and every now and then they came back to tell the little tree how beautiful he was.

Now you can just imagine how happy that little fir tree was. Much, much happier than ever before!

Afterword
Setting the mood for storytelling

According to one story, some parents asked Albert Einstein if more maths would improve their child's intelligence. He answered that, 'If you want your child to be more intelligent, read him fairytales. If you want your child to be wise, read him more fairytales!'

Fairytales have existed for almost as long as time itself. However, this book is about one of the greatest stories ever told, a story that belongs to the hearts of all of us, from birth to old age.

The Christmas stories in this book have delighted children in our kindergartens every year since 1967. We told the stories in the Advent time leading up to Christmas, and also when we returned after the New Year holidays. We performed the Nativity play (The Christmas Story in Verse and Song) annually for the parents of our kindergartens, with the other short stories, to lead the children up to the final performance, and it was adapted to engage from fifteen to sixty children. The words and stories have stood the test of time and have spread to many homes and kindergartens around the world. We used these stories for our own children when they were young, for our grandchildren and hopefully for eventual great-grandchildren. Creating a Nativity scene to go with the stories enhances the whole festival, but the stories can also stand quite freely in their own enchantment.

These stories are best kept for evening or bedtime, with repetitions during the day when requested and when the mood is right. The Advent stories lead to the main story which is kept for Christmas Eve, and those following lead through the holy nights and even further. If there is a Nativity scene, then the baby can be there in the crib on Christmas morning as a surprise when the children awake.

Creating the mood

Of course, it is best to tell or read the stories by candlelight, either in bed or in front of the Nativity scene. The mood should be reverent and quiet. Because children in the first seven years learn through the medium of imitation, it means that the adult must create this special mood within themselves first. Preparation is all important. The hustle and bustle and stress of daily life should be put aside, and an inner peace created. What works well, of course, is softly singing a carol which the children know and so can join in. Whether the adult can sing in tune or not makes no difference as their voice is still loved by their children. The lighting of the candle(s) can be ceremonious because children thrive on repetitive ritual. A special larger candle can be reserved for when the Jesus child is born. It is important for children to learn to anticipate, to have to wait for something special, particularly in these days of instant gratification. Waiting until they are 'old enough' to light the candle themselves, or to wait for the 'baby' candles to be lit, are helpful rituals which children look forward to.

Your storytelling voice can be quiet, slow and the consonants clear. There should be preferably no interruptions, so all electronic devices must be turned completely off, not just on 'silent' mode. This is a 'holy', special time and a lifetime gift to your children which will be carried on through the generations.

After the story, singing and blowing out of the candles, it is sleep-time, with the same reverent mood taken into sleep. All repetitive routines and rituals become habit, and habit is deeply ingrained. Having a bedtime ritual and routine from the start helps to embed sleep patterns and aid what can often be a tricky transition time.

The same story can be repeated many times as children love repetition, and the content of the stories is soul-nourishment for the child, as it is also for adults. When Estelle's father-in-law, an industrialist and chairman of the Board of Commerce and Industry, suffered a heart attack and was bedridden, she gave him the complete book of *Grimm's Fairytales* to read – much to his amusement! After a few days it became his favourite bedtime book. He said that it helped to clarify his mind by lifting him into another realm.

Whether it is a fairytale, a fable or nature story, it can be better to tell the story to the child instead of reading it. Preparation of the story by the adult is important as it engages the will. You become familiar with it, learn to accept it as it is, deepen your understanding of it, and you create mental pictures in order to help remember it. Every child who listens to a story is lifted into the realm of fantasy, which is so necessary for the development of their imagination. It is the listening that activates the imagination, and each time they listen is a new experience, no matter how many times they hear the story. Listening allows us to make our own pictures, so that our own internal creativity is engaged. (Once a child said, 'Can I see that film you told us yesterday?') Note Einstein's quote at the beginning, where he says that fairytales will teach your child to become 'intelligent'. He did not say 'clever'. Intelligence is alive, imaginative and creative.

Children listen in different ways, according to their age. The little ones like to be curled up on your lap, tucked up in bed, or watching you. They may listen with awe in silence, join in with any repetition, or even correct you (the six-year-old) when you make a mistake in the telling! It is important that the stories told are age-appropriate. For the toddler it is best to begin with stories about your family or something taken from your past days, then progress to stories about animals, or other nature stories, and only later to fairytales. There are simple fairytales, such as the Gingerbread Man or the Porridge Pot, which are suitable for younger children, or those like Cinderella, which are only suitable for those over five or six years old.

Fairytales

Rudolf Steiner once said that, 'The human soul has an inextinguishable need to have the substance of fairytales flow through its veins, just as the body needs to have nourishing substances circulate through it.' So there is untold wisdom within fairytales which adults sometimes find difficult to discover. But children need no explanation, they just 'know'. Modern intellect sometimes feels that some fairytales are too cruel and so they have been changed, for instance hiding Red Riding Hood and her Grandmother in the cupboard, with the story ending with them dancing with the wolf! (Giving what they think is a happy ending.) This is exactly what is happening in most parts of the world today – we are dancing with the wolf (greed). We have to develop the courage of the hunter in order to free ourselves from the wolf-qualities which surround us on all sides. If the child is told the original story, they understand it on a much deeper and imaginative level. They do not have our adult mind or fears. So, in telling the fairytale it is important not to arouse fear by using drama in the voice but to understand that there is fear in every human soul. We can learn to deal with and overcome whatever horrors we may meet in life through fairytales.

All the soul qualities that we find in these stories are those which we find in ourselves. No-one is entirely free of greed, envy, anger, fear or the other negative qualities which one finds, for instance, in the witch. They are there to be overcome with the courage of the prince, the princess or the hunter. The overcoming of evil, the courage, and the sometimes cleverness used by the heroes in these fairytales speaks deeply to children on a different level, and thus gives them strength throughout their lives. This is particularly necessary today when courage, positivity, strength and a belief in the good is so needed.

Sharing together

Of course reading stories together and showing the child pictures is also a wonderful experience. It can also demonstrate how to care for and handle books properly. To see parents enjoy reading will give their children a love for books as well, and later, when children are old enough to read for themselves, they can share the stories, perhaps with younger siblings. The quiet, special and gentle mood that you have established for storytime will be deeply ingrained, and they will treasure this special moment. In the same way that we repeat stories we learn by heart and tell at bedtime, so also should sharing a special picture book be repeated, for then it becomes a favourite. The children memorise the story after a while, and will 'read' it with you. Reading the pictures and making up stories about the pictures can be also wonderful. A beautifully illustrated book often has so much more appearing in the pictures than in the actual words, so you are stimulating a creative and imaginative response in a child.

We hope that you enjoy these Advent and Christmas stories and that they will be passed down through the generations in the same way that they have in our families. Also, we hope that they will be turned into scenes, accompany puppet plays, be acted, sung, performed by all ages, and over many years; that they will be accompanied by singing and creative activity; and that they will bring a mood of quiet, of anticipation, of joy, of wholeness and of love – all of which were brought to the world with the birth of the Christ child so long ago.

Janni Nicol

About the authors

Estelle Bryer

Estelle Bryer is a founder teacher of the Waldorf School Movement in South Africa, where she taught in Cape Town for 43 years as kindergarten teacher, eurythmy teacher and eurythmy therapist. She specialises in kindergarten eurythmy.

She has lectured widely to diverse audiences, teacher training centres and professional groups. She is also a published author of children's stories, puppet plays and a guidance book for teachers on movement in the kindergarten.

Estelle is best known as South Africa's foremost puppeteer for children, having performed solo to more than three quarters of a million children and adults over the past 50 years. In 1992 she established the only permanent puppet theatre in the country, which still performs weekly to the public. She is also Janni's mother.

Janni Nicol

Janni Nicol trained as a Steiner kindergarten teacher in 1969. Since then she taught in various kindergartens, is the founder teacher of the Rosebridge Kindergartens and was instrumental in founding the Cambridge Steiner School, UK, has worked in marketing and PR, published articles and become a puppeteer. She is the Early Years Representative for the Steiner Waldorf Schools Fellowship, UK, and works with the International Association of Steiner Waldorf Early Childhood (IASWECE).

She publishes and edits *KINDLING* (Journal for Steiner Waldorf Early Childhood), lectures internationally on many aspects of Steiner Early Years education, and puppetry. She is the author of many books on Steiner education and creative play. This is her third book with her mother, Estelle Bryer.

Other books from Hawthorn Press

Healing Stories for Challenging Behaviour
Susan Perrow

Susan Perrow is a story doctor. She writes, collects and documents stories that offer a therapeutic journey for the storyteller and listener – a positive, imaginative way of healing difficult situations.
Healing Stories for Challenging Behaviour is richly illustrated with lively anecdotes drawn from parents and teachers who have discovered how the power of story can help resolve a range of common childhood behaviours and situations such as separation anxiety, bullying, sibling rivalry, nightmares and grieving.
ISBN: 978-1-903458-78-5234 × 156mm; paperback

Therapeutic Storytelling
101 Healing Stories for Children
Susan Perrow

This treasury of healing stories addresses a range of issues – from unruly behaviour to grieving, anxiety, lack of confidence, b ullying, teasing, nightmares, intolerance, inappropriate talk, toileting, bedwetting and much more. The stories also have the potential for nurturing positive values.
Susan Perrow M.Ed runs therapeutic storytelling workshops from China to Africa, Europe to America and across her own sun-burnt land of Australia. Her acclaimed first b ook, *H e aling S tories f or Challenging Behaviour*, has been translated into several languages.
ISBN: 978-1-907359-15-6; 234 × 159mm; paperback

Stories to Light the Night
A Grief and Loss Collection for Children,
Families and Communities
Susan Perrow

Stories and words have therapeutic potential. They can strengthen us, help to reframe things, and help make meaning. These 94 stories cover many kinds of loss, from the death of a family member or pet to the loss of health, home, country or place. As well as original stories from Susan Perrow, there are stories by writers from different countries and cultures worldwide.
ISBN: 978-1-912480-27-2; 234 × 156mm; paperback

Fairytales, Families & Forests
Storytelling with young children
Georgiana Keable and Dawne McFarlane

Fairytales, Families and Forests encourages parents and teachers of very young children to tell stories in their family or pre-school. There is a chapter for each year of the child's life from birth to seven years, with age specific stories, verses, games and how to use them, including the use of sign language and special needs.
ISBN: 978-1-912480-38-8; 228 x 186mm; paperback

The Natural Storyteller
Wildlife Tales for Telling
Georgiana Keable

The Natural Storyteller is a vibrant invitation to embrace a world of stories all about nature, animals and plants – and our relationship with them. It includes story maps, brain-teasing riddles, story skeletons and adventures to make a tale your own. This diverse collection of stories will nurture active literacy skills, and help form an essential bond with nature. The Natural Storyteller recently won first place in the Green Books/Environmental category of the Purple Dragonfly Book Awards.
ISBN: 978-1-907359-80-4; 228 x 186mm; paperback

Storytelling with Children
Nancy Mellon

Telling stories awakens wonder and creates special occasions with children, whether it is bedtime, around the fire or on rainy days. Encouraging you to spin golden tales, Nancy Mellon shows how you can become a confident storyteller and enrich your family with the power of story. Find the tale you want from Nancy's rich story-cupboard.
Nancy Mellon runs a School for Therapeutic Storytelling and lives in New Hampshire.

ISBN: 978-1-903458-08-2; 216 x 138mm; paperback

Making the Children's Year
Seasonal Waldorf Crafts with Children
Marije Rowling

Bringing inspiration and ideas to a modern readership, this book is packed with all kinds of crafts, from papercrafting to building dens. From beginners to experienced crafters, this book is a gift for parents and adults seeking to make toys that will inspire children and provide an alternative to throwaway culture.
ISBN: 978-1-907359-69-9; 250 × 200mm; paperback

The Children's Forest
Stories & songs, wild food, crafts & celebrations all year round
Dawn Casey, Anna Richardson, Helen d'Ascoli

A rich and abundant treasury in celebration of the outdoors, this book encourages children's natural fascination with the forest and its inhabitants. Full of games, facts, celebrations, craft activities, recipes, foraging, stories and Forest School skills, this book is ideal for ages 5-12, but it will also be enjoyed by adults, families and younger children.
ISBN: 978-1-907359-91-0; 250 × 200mm; paperback with flaps

Festivals, Family and Food
Guide to seasonal celebration
Diana Carey, Judy Large

This family favourite is a unique, well-loved source of stories, recipes, things to make, activities, poems, songs and festivals.
Each festival such as Christmas, Candlemas and Martinmas has its own, well-illustrated chapter. There are also sections on Birthdays, Rainy Days, Convalescence and a birthday Calendar. The perfect present for a family, it explores the numerous festivals that children love celebrating.
ISBN: 978-0-950706-23-8; 250 × 200mm; paperback

Making Peg Dolls
Margaret Bloom

Coming from the Waldorf handcraft tradition, these irresistible dolls encourage creative play and promote the emotional and imaginative development of young children. Peg dolls can be made from natural materials to reflect the seasonal cycle, favourite fairytales and festivals from around the world. Inside this book you will find patterns for creating bluebirds & butterflies, flowers & fairytale figures, gnomes, winter angels and more.
ISBN: 978-1-907359-77-4; 198 × 208mm; paperback

Simplicity Parenting
Using the power of less to raise happy, secure children
Kim John Payne

This new and revised UK edition of the popular US #1 provides tried, tested and doable answers to the rapid increase in anxiety in childhood and the ever-increasing need for balance in family life.
Here are four simple steps for decluttering, quieting, and soothing family dynamics so that children can thrive at school, get along with peers, and nurture well-being. Using the extraordinary power of less, Kim John Payne, one of the world's leading Steiner-Waldorf educators, offers novel ways to help children feel calmer, happier, and more secure.
ISBN: 978-1-912480-03-6; 234 × 156mm; paperback

Ordering Books

If you have difficulty ordering Hawthorn Press books from a bookshop, you can order direct from our website **www.hawthornpress.com**, or from our distributors:
UK: BookSource: Tel: (0845) 370 0067, Email: orders@booksource.net
USA: Steinerbooks, Tel: 703-661-1594, Email: service@steinerbooks.org

Hawthorn Press

www.hawthornpress.com